FOR AUDIENCES 18+ ONLY

This book is intended for adults only. Spanking and other sexual
activities represented in this book are fantasies only, intended for
adults.

MATED TO THE BEAST

BEAST

GRACE GOODWIN

Published by Stormy Night Publications and Design, LLC.
www.StormyNightPublications.com

Cover design by Korey Mae Johnson
www.koreymaejohnson.com

Images by The Killion Group and 123RF/Dmitriy Denysov

1st Print Edition. August 2016

ISBN-13: 978-1536875096

ISBN-10: 1536875090

CHAPTER ONE

Sarah, Interstellar Bride Processing Center, Earth

My back was pressed into something smooth and hard. Against my front was something equally hard, but hot as I stroked my palms over it. I could feel the heartbeat beneath the sweat-soaked skin, hear the rumbling of pleasure in his chest. His teeth nipped at the spot where my shoulder met my neck, the sensation sharp and with a hint of pain. A knee nudged my thighs apart and my toes barely touched the floor. I was pinned in such a *good* way between a man, a very big and eager man, and a wall.

Hands slid over my waist and higher to cup my breasts, to pluck at my already hard nipples. My body melted at his skilled touch and I was glad for the wall and his secure hold. His hands moved higher, lifting my arms up until he gripped both of my wrists in one very large, strong hand and held them in place over my head. I was well and truly pinned. I didn't care. I should, for I didn't like to be manhandled, but this… oh, God, this was different.

This was fucked-up-against-a-wall goodness.

I didn't want to think about being in control, of knowing what would come next. I just knew that whatever he did I

1

wanted more. He was wild, untamed, and aggressive. The press of his thick cock was hot against my inner thigh.

"Please," I whimpered.

"Your pussy's so wet it's dripping on my thigh."

I could feel how slick I was, my clit pulsing, my inner walls clenching down in eager anticipation.

"Do you want my cock to fill you up?"

"Yes," I cried, nodding my head against the hard surface.

"You said earlier you would never submit."

"I will. I will," I gasped, going against everything I knew. I didn't submit to anyone. I stood on my own two feet, defended myself with my fists or sharp words. I didn't let *anyone* tell me what to do. I'd had enough of that with my family and I wouldn't take it anymore. But this man… with him, I would give him anything, even my submission.

"You'll do as I say?" His voice was rough and deep, a mixture of dominant and aroused male.

"I will, just please, *please*, fuck me."

"Ah, I love to hear those words from your mouth. But you know you're going to have to soothe my beast, my fever. I won't just fuck you once. I'll fuck you again and again, hard and rough, just as you need it. I'll make you come so many times you won't remember any name but mine."

I moaned then. "Do it. Take me." His words were so dirty that I should have been mortified, but they only made me hotter. "Fill me up. I can soothe your fever. I'm the only one."

I didn't even know what that meant, but I *felt* that it was true. I was the only one who could ease the anxious rage inside him that I could sense lurking beneath his gentle touch, his soft lips. Fucking was an outlet for his intensity and it was my job, my role, to help. Not that it would be a burden; I was desperate for him to fuck me. Perhaps I had the fever, too.

He held me up as if I weighed nothing, my back arched by his hold on my wrists, my breasts thrust out in offering as I squirmed to get closer, to force him to fill me.

"Put your legs around me. Open up, give me what I want. Offer it to me." He bit down gently at the curve of my shoulder and I whimpered in need as his massive chest rubbed my sensitive nipples and his thigh nudged higher, forcing me to ride him, pushing against my sensitive clit in a relentless assault meant to make me lose control.

Using his hold on me for leverage, I lifted my legs and bucked against him until I felt the head of his big cock at my entrance. As soon as I had him where I wanted him, I crossed my ankles just above the curve of his well-muscled ass and tried to pull him closer, to impale myself, but he was too big, too strong, and I moaned in frustration.

"Say it, mate, as I fill you with my cock. Say my name. Say whose cock is filling you. Say the name of the only one you will submit to. Say it."

His cock nudged in, spreading my pussy lips wide, stretching me open. I could feel the hardness of it, the heat of it. I could smell the musky scent of my arousal, of fucking. I could feel his mouth sucking on the sensitive skin of my neck. I could feel the steel-like strength of his grip where he held me in place and the solid wall behind me, allowing me no escape from the dominance of his thrusting body. I could feel his powerful bulk as I clenched him with my thighs. I felt the shift of the muscles in his ass as he thrust into me.

I tilted my head back and cried out his name, the one name that meant everything to me.

"Miss Mills."

The voice was soft, timid even, not *his*. I ignored it and thought of the way his cock was filling me up. I'd never been stretched so fully before and the slight burn of it mixed with the pleasure of that flared head sliding over the most sensitive places deep inside me.

"Miss Mills."

I felt a hand on my shoulder. Cold. Small. It wasn't *his* hand because his hands had moved to my ass in the dream, clenching and squeezing as he drove deep, pinning me to the wall.

I startled awake and tugged my arm away from the clammy touch of a stranger. Blinking a few times, I realized the woman before me was Warden Morda. It was not the man in the dream. Oh, God, it had been a dream.

I gasped and tried to catch my breath as I stared at her.

She was reality. Warden Morda was with me in this room. I wasn't being fucked by a dominant male with a huge cock and the words of a demanding lover. She had the expression of a constipated cat and it was perhaps the look on my face that had her taking a step back. How dare she interrupt *that* dream? The best sex I'd ever had didn't even come close. Holy hell, that was a hot dream. I'd never had head banging, slammed up against the wall kind of sex before, but I wanted it now. My inner walls clenched, remembering what that cock felt like. My fingers itched to grab his shoulders again. I wanted to lock my ankles about his waist, dig my heels into his ass.

This was insane, a sex dream. Now, here. God, it was almost mortifying if it hadn't been so real. No, it *was* mortifying because I was supposed to be processed for the coalition front lines, not a job as a porn star. I assumed the processing meant a medical check, birth control implant, perhaps some mental health assessment. I'd been in the military before, but not in space. How different could it be? What kind of processing did the coalition have to force me into a dream porno? Was it because I was a woman? Did they want to ensure I wouldn't jump a fellow soldier? That was ridiculous, but what else could be the reason for that steamy hot dream?

"What?" I barked, still angry at being wrenched away from such pleasure, embarrassed she caught me when I was so emotionally vulnerable.

She flinched, clearly unaccustomed to the rough edges of new recruits. Odd, since she dealt with them on a daily basis. She *had* said she was new in her role here at the processing center, but how new was undetermined. Just my luck, this was probably her first day.

"I'm sorry to have disturbed you." Her voice was meek. She reminded me of a mouse. Drab brown hair, straight and long. No makeup, her uniform making her appear sallow. "Your testing is complete."

Frowning, I glanced down at myself. I felt like I was at the doctor's office with the hospital-style gown with a red logo repeated in a pattern on the scratchy material. The chair was like one at the dentist's, but the wrist restraints were an unwelcome touch. I yanked on them, testing their strength, but they would not yield. I was trapped. Not a feeling I enjoyed, at all. It made me think of the dream where he'd pinned my hands over my head, but that, that I'd enjoyed. A lot. Except he'd made me tell him I wanted to submit, to give control to him. It made no sense because I *hated* giving control to anyone. I drove when I went out with friends. I organized the birthday parties. I used to buy the groceries for my family. I had a father and three brothers, all bossy. While they'd raised me to be just as bossy as they were, they never allowed me to tell them what to do. They pestered me, teased me, scared away any guy even remotely interested in me. They'd gone off to the military and I'd followed. I craved control as much as they did.

Now, with these damn restraints, I felt trapped. Pinned down with no escape. I glared at the warden.

Her shoulders went slack, shrinking her size another inch or two.

"My testing is over? Aren't you interested in my accuracy with firearms? Hand-to-hand combat? Piloting skills?"

She licked her lips and cleared her throat. "Your... um... skills are impressive, I'm sure, but unless they were a part of the testing you just finished, then... no."

My skills in battle were plenty, for I had years of experience, probably more than most coalition recruits. My understanding was that all tests were conducted via simulations like the one I'd just endured, which was odd, but perhaps faster than soldiers proving their worth on the firing range or in an actual aircraft. Was the sex dream some kind of new test? I wasn't a nympho, but I also wouldn't turn down a hot guy if the right one came along. But I knew there was a difference between the bedroom and the battlefield. Why would they care what my sexual proclivities were? Did they think a human woman would be unable to resist a smoking hot alien? Hell, I'd been around hot alpha males most of my life. Resistance was not a problem.

Or were they trying to prove there was something wrong with me that I had conjured up a woman being dominated and pinned against a wall by an eager and well-endowed guy? He hadn't been forceful. I hadn't feared him. I'd longed for him. I'd *begged* for him. There had been no explosions, unless you considered the fact that I'd almost come when he'd bottomed out deep inside me. I clenched my core muscles down again, the vividness of the dream causing me to long for the heat of the huge man's seed filling me.

It was my turn to clear my throat.

A crisp knock on the door had the warden spinning on her rubber-soled heels.

In walked another woman in an identical uniform, but she wore it with much more confidence and a knowledgeable demeanor.

"Miss Mills, I am Warden Egara. I see you have finished your testing." Warden Egara had dark brown hair, gray eyes, and the bearing and posture of a dancer. Her shoulders were straight, her body trim and upright. Everything about her screamed educated, confident, refined. The exact opposite of the neighborhood I'd grown up in. The warden glanced at the tablet she carried with her. I assumed the nod of her head indicated she was satisfied, but her expression was carefully schooled and gave nothing away.

I wished for half her restraint as I felt a fierce scowl cover my face. "Is there a reason I am shackled to this chair?"

The last thing I remembered was sitting across from the little mouse—who now practically cowered next to the confident warden—and taking a small pill from her hand. I washed it down with a paper cup full of water. I was now naked beneath my gown—I could feel my bare ass against the hard plastic—and restrained. If I were to be dressed in anything at all, it shouldn't be this ridiculous medical gown, but a warrior's uniform for my induction as a coalition fighter.

The warden glanced at me and offered an efficient smile. Everything about her seemed to be professional, unlike the mouse.

"Some women have strong reactions to the testing. The restraints are for your own safety."

"Then you wouldn't mind removing them now?"

I felt out of control with my arms pinned. If there was danger of some kind, I could kick an attacker since my legs were free, but they'd certainly get an eyeful when I lifted my leg.

"Not until we are finished. Per protocol," she added, as if that would make a difference.

She took a seat at the table across from me, the mouse easing into a seat beside her.

"We have some standard questions in order to proceed, Miss Mills."

I tried not to roll my eyes, but knew the military was a stickler for paperwork and organization. I shouldn't be surprised that a military organization made up of over two hundred member planets had some hoops I would have to jump through. My induction into the U.S. Army had taken days of paperwork, and that was for a small country, on one small blue planet out of hundreds. Hell, I'd be lucky if the aliens' coalition process didn't take two months.

"All right," I replied, eager to get this done. I had a brother to find and time was wasting. Every second I was stuck here on Earth was another second my crazy, hell-raising brother might do something stupid and get himself killed.

"Your name is Sarah Mills, correct?"

"Yes."

"You are not married."

"No."

"No children?"

Now I did roll my eyes. I wouldn't volunteer for active duty military service, in outer space, battling the terrifying Hive if I had kids. I was about to sign on the dotted line for a two-year deployment and would never leave children behind. Not even for the promise I'd made my father on his deathbed.

"No. I do not have any children."

"Very well. You've been matched to the planet Atlan."

I frowned. "That's nowhere near the front lines." I *did* know where the fighting was happening because my two brothers, John and Chris, had died out there in space and my youngest brother, Seth, was still fighting.

"That's correct." She looked over my shoulder and had a vague stare of someone who was thinking. "If my geography is correct, Atlan is about three lightyears away from the closest active Hive outpost."

"Then why am I going there?"

It was the warden's turn to frown, her gaze focused on my face. "Because that is where your matched mate will come from."

My mouth fell open and I stared at the woman, my eyes so heavy with shock it felt like they were about to pop out of my head. "My *mate*? Why would I want a mate?"

CHAPTER TWO

Sarah

My surprised tone and blatantly shocked expression were clearly new to the woman. She flicked a glance at the mouse, then back at me. "Well, um... because you are here for the Interstellar Bride Program processing and testing. Sometimes a woman takes longer to recover from the testing and can wake... confused. However, no woman has ever forgotten the reason she was here. I find your line of questioning worrisome. Miss Mills, are you feeling all right?" She turned to the mouse. "Call downstairs. I think she might need a repeat on the brain scan."

"I do not need a scan." I sat up then and fought the restraints, but I couldn't move. My struggles had both women sitting up straight in their chairs as I continued. "I'm feeling fine. I think she—" I opened my fist and pointed at the mouse, who was now biting her lip and clenching the edge of the table, "—made a big mistake."

Warden Egara remained unflappable as her fingers flew over the tablet. A minute passed, then another. She looked up at me. "You are Sarah Mills and you have volunteered to be a bride in the Interstellar Bride Program."

9

Laughter bubbled up and escaped. It probably *was* a good thing I was restrained. "No way. I'm the last person who needs to be matched to a man. I grew up with three brothers and an overprotective daddy who were all neck deep in my personal life. They were bossy as hell and scared off any guy who even *thought* about me in any kind of sexual way." I did figure out how to keep *some* things secret, including men, but what my family didn't know hadn't hurt them. "Why on Earth would I need a mate?"

"He wouldn't be *on* Earth," the mouse piped up.

Whipping her head around, Warden Egara glared at the mouse and I was quite impressed. Not many civilian women I knew had the whole death stare down. The warden, however, was a pro.

"Then why are you here?" The warden returned her attention to me, her head tilted to the side as if I were a puzzle she was trying to solve.

"I'm now wondering where *here* is, but I volunteered for Earth's contingent as a coalition fighter."

"But you're a woman," the mouse countered, her eyes wide.

I glanced down my body as I replied. I was strong, not thin. My bones were heavy and I'd spent nearly as many hours in the weight room as most of the guys in my unit. Despite all the hours of training, I was still curvy, with lush hips and full breasts, and could not be mistaken for a man. "Yes, my brothers took great pleasure in pointing that out to me."

I thought of them, two now gone and one up in space fighting the Hive. I'd hated their pestering at the time, but with John and Chris now dead, I'd give anything—including fighting the Hive myself—to hear Seth tease me again. Seth was still out there, somewhere. And I was going to find him and bring him home. That's what my dad wanted, what he'd made me promise I'd do before he died.

"But there aren't any women who've volunteered." The mouse fidgeted, her left knee bouncing up and down like a springboard.

"That's not true," the warden replied, her voice crisp and angry. "This is your second day in your role and therefore you are ignorant of many things. There have been Earth women who volunteered to fight the Hive, just not many. Miss Mills, I believe an apology is in order."

"Thank you." My shoulders slumped in relief and I felt like I could breathe again. I didn't want or need a mate. I didn't want to go to Atlan. I both wanted and needed to go kill the things that had killed my two brothers. My father would roll over in his grave if I walked away from this war and pretended to be a weak, scared female who needed a man to take care of her. That wasn't how I was raised. My father and brothers made sure I knew how to take care of myself, expected more from me. "When do I leave? I'm ready to go fight the Hive."

I knew most rational women would have thought I was insane. Who would turn down a perfect match, a mate who would be totally and completely devoted to me for the rest of my life, a strong man who could give me children and a home, for battle and most likely death?

I guess that would be me.

"You have been assigned to Atlan," she clarified. "The testing has been done. Based on your psychological profile and testing by the matching program, your mate will be selected from available males on the planet Atlan. They do things a bit different there—"

"No. But—" I interrupted, but she wasn't finished.

She sighed and held up her hand to stall any more argument from me. "You'll be transported off planet without your consent. I assume I do not have it."

"No. You do not," I replied, very clearly. "I don't need to have an alien man, some... *mate* telling me what to do."

"You're going to have a commanding officer, most likely a man, tell you exactly what to do for the next two years," the mouse countered.

She had a point, but I wasn't going to tell her that.

Besides, there was a big difference between a mate who, according to coalition laws, would be legally allowed to boss me around for the rest of my life and a commanding officer who would be out of my life in two years. "I'll do whatever it takes to find my brother. The *only* brother I have left alive after this fight with the Hive. I made a promise to my father and *nothing* is going to stop me from keeping my word."

Both women looked at me with wide eyes, probably surprised by my vehemence. I wasn't fucking around. I wanted to find Seth and I wanted to kill as many Hive as I could for taking away John and Chris. The Hive hadn't *actually* killed my dad, but the grief of my brothers' deaths certainly helped finish him off.

"Very well," the warden replied, swiping her finger over the tablet, which released my restraints. "Since I do not have your consent to be a bride, you are free to go to the Interstellar Battle Battalion's testing center and begin your processing so they can get you sworn in."

I spoke as I rubbed my wrists. "So, all of this was a waste? I have to start over, over there?"

She sighed. "I'm afraid so. I'm sorry."

"As long as we've got the whole mate problem straightened out, it's fine." I felt better knowing the reason behind the sex dream. For a minute, I'd wondered if I had some repressed, kinky woman I didn't recognize hiding inside my head. I was relieved to discover that it wasn't my fault. I hadn't done anything to make that sexual imagery bubble to the surface.

I swiveled in the chair and put my bare feet on the cold floor. My legs were shaking but I refused to think about the reason. Why was having a bossy mate more frightening to me than battling pitiless, inhuman, alien cyborgs?

Well, for starters, if a cyborg pissed me off, I could blow his head off and walk away. But a mate? Well, he'd make me angry and I'd be stuck with him forever, festering like a volcano, never able to blow... And, God knew, I had a temper. It had gotten me into trouble more than once. But it had also saved my life. Seth used to tease me about it, saying I would end up immortal because I was just too stubborn to die.

"I will escort you personally to ensure you are indeed in the right place this time." The warden spoke to me, but she was looking at the cringing mouse. "And that *all* protocols have been followed to the letter."

I offered the mouse a small smile. "Don't be too hard on her," I replied. "She's new. And I had an amazing dream."

Shit, had I ever. If the guy I would have been matched to was anything like the big, aggressive lover in the dream… the thought made my nipples harden.

The warden lifted a brow. "It's not too late to change your mind, Miss Mills. You should know that was not a dream, it was processing center data experienced by another bride during her claiming ceremony with a male from Atlan."

"Processing data?"

The warden flushed, her cheeks turning a bright pink as I tried to wrap my mind about what that meant, *exactly*.

"Yes. When she is sent off world, a bride is implanted with a Neurostim Unit right here. The same for coalition fighters." She lifted her finger and tapped the bony protrusion of her skull just above her temple. "It will help you learn and adapt to all the languages in the Interstellar Coalition."

"I'd be able to talk to anyone?"

"Yes. But that's not all." Her eyes darted away, then back to mine. "When a bride is claimed by her mate, the sensory data, what she sees, hears, and… feels," the warden cleared her throat, "is recorded and used to mentally stimulate and process future brides to determine their suitability for that planet's men and customs."

Holy shit. "So, it wasn't a dream. I was reliving someone else's *memory*? That really happened?"

The warden smiled. "Oh, yes. Exactly as you

experienced it."

"To another woman?"

"Yes."

Wow. I had no idea what to do with that knowledge. Did that mean that all men from Atlan were as dominant as the one in the dream? He'd spoken of a fever, a rage that only I—the woman in the dream—could tame. Did he mean he was hot for her? If that was what a dream felt like, I could only imagine how amazing it would have been if it had been real. God, that man, he was unlike any guy I'd ever met on Earth. That dream had been hotter than any experience I'd had actually taking a man to bed.

But it *was* a dream, at least for me. I shouldn't linger on it. It was a mistake. I was going to fight for the coalition. I was going to find Seth. I didn't have time to be distracted by lust. It was pure, mindless lust. I was thinking about killing cyborgs, and yet my nipples were still hard. Totally unacceptable. Duty first. My bottled-up libido would have to wait until after my brother was home safe. I had to find him, fight with him, and finish up our terms of service. *Then* we could go home.

I looked up to find the warden watching me closely. "You can still change your mind, Miss Mills. You will be matched to a warrior from Atlan. He'll be yours completely, your psychological profiles and preferences aligned. He will be totally devoted, loyal, and perfect for you in every way."

I remembered the hard thrust of the man's cock, the way I'd moaned and squirmed against the wall as he took me. The powerful lure of being wanted, desired to a point of mindless fucking flooded me with longing. I could have that. I could have one of those big, rough lovers all to myself—

No. No way. I wouldn't let my hormones turn me into an idiot. I had a plan, a purpose. I needed to find Seth. I did not *need* a hot man with a huge cock that could make me come just from taking me hard and deep. I sighed. Need? No. But *want…*

Damn. Focus! *Duty first.* I would not be weak. I had one brother left. One.

"I don't want a mate, warden. I simply need to get to the front lines and fight beside my brother. I promised my father I'd watch over him and make sure he comes home."

She sighed, clearly disappointed. "Very well."

• • • • • • •

Dax, Battleship Brekk, Sector 592, The Front

"Get this soldier matched and mated," my commanding officer bellowed, shoving me into the medical station onboard the Battleship Brekk the moment the doors to the room slid open.

All workers spun around as the booming order echoed off the hard, sterile surfaces of medical exam tables and smooth, glass screens that covered nearly every square inch of the walls. Across their glossy surfaces flowed an unending stream of medical data, bioscans, and testing results of the patients on display.

A man in the gray uniform worn by the medical support staff dashed forward. "We will need you to schedule an appointment—"

"Now!" Commander Deek shouted. "Unless you want an Atlan berserker in beast form tearing apart this ship."

The medical officer jumped a foot and nodded his head as a doctor hurried to take over. She was wearing the formal green uniform of all high-ranking doctors, but she was small and delicate, nowhere near big enough to stop me if the frenzy I felt building within were to break free. I fought back the fury in deference to the tiny female, thankful the huge Prillon doctor I spied on the opposite side of the medical station wasn't standing before me now. My reaction to the woman was telling. Commander Deek was right. I needed a mate to calm the beast. Didn't mean I liked the idea.

"It can wait," I grumbled, not eager to be the center of

everyone's attention. The thick rumble of my voice was further evidence of how close I was to the edge of control. I'd been feeling the call to mate for weeks and had ignored it. There was always another battle, another Hive outpost to destroy. I had a job to do, and my body was no longer allowing me to do it. Instead, my cock and my mind had become tuned to just one need: the need to mate, to rut, to fuck until I couldn't see straight. I needed a mate to calm the beast, or the beast would consume me until I was nothing but a mindless animal. And now, everyone on board this ship would know just how badly I needed to get laid. Mate or die. That was the way for an Atlan male. We were too powerful to be allowed to go feral. If I didn't mate soon, the other Atlan warriors would be forced to execute me, as was their right.

I knew all of this, and yet I had truly believed I could hold off the mating fever just a few more weeks. I'd be home, then. My service to the coalition military served. I'd be free to choose any woman on the home world. I'd be a victor, sought after and fought over by the smartest, most beautiful, most desirable females. If I could just make it home.

"I wouldn't have to scare the staff if you had told me your mating fever was upon you," he countered, releasing his grip on my shoulder.

"I don't see what that has to do with my performance in the last raid. I've got it under control."

"You rushed straight into our line of fire and singlehandedly took out an entire squadron of Hive scouts. The last two you did not simply shoot. No, your beast demanded their heads be ripped from their bodies." He crossed his arms and scowled at me. "I'm not some ignorant Trion commander. I'm Atlan. I know the signs, Dax. Your beast nearly claimed you out there today. It's time."

I glanced down at my upturned palms. I was just as deadly as any other Atlan, except for the fact that I'd never had such a fiery rage take me over. The Atlan were feared in battle, known to be cold and calculating, and very powerful. No Atlan warrior—at least none free of mating fever—would dismantle a Hive fighter—or three—with his bare hands. It would be judged an inefficient use of energy. But today, I'd laid eyes on my enemies and had an uncontrollable need... this primal *urge* to rip them in half. And so I did.

I'd noticed the intensity of my hatred growing over the past few weeks, but I'd refused to think about mating fever as the reason. I was already two years older than most men when their mating fever struck and had simply tried to forget all about it.

"You should be thanking me for my kill count today, not matching me to an alien."

He pushed me in the direction the doctor indicated, toward another staff member who had readied a testing station for me. Commander Deek thanked her and shoved me toward the chair once she wandered off to attend to her other patients. "I'll thank you after you're mated and I know I don't have to execute you for losing control." His grin then was one I expected, the shared satisfaction of victory. "I admit, I will be sorry to see you go."

A man whose mating fever was upon him was immediately relieved of duty and sent home to Atlan to take a mate. His term of service fighting the Hive was over. A man's new job was to procreate, to breed his new mate like the beast he was until she carried his child.

Retiring and raising a family while there were still active Hive outposts to fight? No. That, I had no desire to do. I belonged on the front lines of battle, tearing the heads off my enemies and protecting my people. I didn't need a mate, nor did I desire offspring. I was content with my life as it was. Out here, I was a warrior with purpose. What was I to do with a mate? Follow her around like a lovesick youth, stroking my cock and wasting precious hours trying to convince an alien female not to fear me or my beast? How was I supposed to do that?

When an Atlan turned into a beast, his muscles bulged to nearly twice their size, teeth lengthened into fangs, and the ability to speak was nearly lost. What was an alien female going to do with an Atlan gone berserk?

I needed to go home and find an Atlan female, one I knew wouldn't fear me. A woman I wouldn't fear breaking in half with my giant cock and my need to completely dominate her body, to cover her with my bulk and fuck her until she passed out. Resistance riled my beast, and in rut of a mating fever, any rebellion or disobedience from a female would be harshly dealt with. An Atlan female would respond well to my need for control, would grow wet with welcome when I growled at her and would spread her legs wide for my eager cock, knowing that her soft body and wet pussy would tame me in the end. Perhaps she would even allow me to sleep with my head pillowed on her soft thigh, my face next to the sweet scent of her pussy as I dreamed of fucking her again.

But an alien woman? What was she going to expect? A man who daydreamed and wrote love letters and brought her shiny gifts? No. On Atlan, holding a woman's hands locked over her head and fucking her against the wall *was* a love letter. An Atlan warrior's gift to his bride was to tie her down and lick her pussy until her orgasms made her scream and beg to be fucked. My cock swelled at the images in my mind and I shifted, trying to hide my condition from Commander Deek. I glanced at his face, at his raised brow, and conceded defeat. *Mating fever.* I simply could *not* stop thinking about fucking.

"Let me go home. I can find a mate on my own," I replied as I dropped into the exam chair. It was reclined, so I leaned back, crossed my arms over my waist, and stared up at the metal ceiling with a clenched jaw.

"You don't have time to go through a formal courtship on Atlan. That could take months." He took a seat on a stool near the end of the table and looked me straight in the eye. "You'll be dead in a week if you aren't mated. You have no time to court and woo an elite Atlan female and can be placed at the top of the list for a mate. Clearly your fever offers special accommodation and haste."

I gave him a disbelieving gaze, raising my brow. "Court and woo? And who said anything about an elite?" At this point, I'd settle for a prostitute on the outer rim as long as her skin was soft and her pussy was wet.

He rolled his eyes. No warrior returned home to Atlan to anything less than an elite female. Warrior mates were prized possessions on Atlan; wealthy, influential and respected. The available females, and their fathers, would expect a full ritual courtship from me, were I to return home now. I was a ground commander, a warlord in charge of several thousand infantry forces and raiding squadrons. I was not a first year soldier returning home with nothing. The Atlan senate would honor me upon my return with wealth, property, and title.

Commander Deek was right. Even if I transported home today, I wouldn't have an approved mating for months. I didn't have time for formality. I didn't have time to woo and court a soft Atlan female. I needed quick and dirty. I needed a woman I could mount and fuck and dominate now, a woman to bring me back from the edge. Someone soft, serene, gentle, and fertile, as the elite females on Atlan were. A woman who could pet my beast and calm my rage.

He cuffed me on the shoulder when he noticed I no longer paid attention. "Listen, Dax. You will only take a mate once and you need to do it right. Even if you're matched to an alien."

The idea of coming to actually *like* a mate, an *alien* mate, was highly improbable. But I didn't need to fall in love. I just needed to fuck her. Well, not just fuck her, but *bond* with her to satisfy my beast's hunger for touch, for the soothing stroke of a woman's hands on my body. Should be simple enough.

"All right. Get it done," I said, resolved.

Restraints curved up and around my wrists and locked

into place. My inner beast raged at the confinement, but I remained in control. Barely. I knew this was the fastest way to summon a mate and I focused on that fact above all else until the beast stilled within me, watchful but willing to wait.

The medical officer attached probes to my temples and began pressing all kinds of buttons on the screen in the wall behind my head. I ignored him completely. I didn't want a step-by-step analysis or explanation. I wanted it over.

"There will be no pain with the testing, Warlord Dax," the medical officer said, not looking at me but at his screen. "The matching takes into account many factors, including physical compatibility, personality, appearance, sexual needs, repressed fantasies, sexual drive, genetic likelihood of producing viable offspring—"

"Begin, without the blathering."

The man closed his mouth. Commander Deek may have been in charge of the Atlan battle group, but I was a leader in my own right and everyone knew it. Including, it seemed, those in the medical station.

The man flicked his gaze at Commander Deek, who stiffly nodded.

"Very well. Close your eyes..."

· · · · · · ·

I opened my eyes to find Commander Deek looming over me. His stern face held a frown and I wondered just how close he was to his own mating fever. "Maybe you should be the one on the table."

"No," he growled, looking at the medical officer standing behind me. "Was the match made? Or do I need to send Warlord Dax home on the next transport?"

I blinked a few times, trying to recall what the hell had just happened to me. I didn't remember much beyond the needy cries of a woman and the bliss of burying my cock deep inside a warm, wet...

"It's over. The match has been made." The voice came

from beside me and I didn't need to turn my head to know it was the same medical officer who irritated me earlier by talking overly much. But this time, I required an explanation.

"Are you certain you completed the testing?" I barked. "I don't remember anything."

Nothing had happened except I now had vague memories that lingered in the back of my mind, and a painfully hard cock straining to escape my armored pants. I'd been dragged directly from the battlefield to the medical unit, and the hard casing of the ground armor made my erection incredibly painful. With my hands restrained, it wasn't as if I could even shift my damn cock to a less agonizing position.

The medical officer stepped over to stand near my hip, where I could see him. His voice sounded vaguely bored and routine. "You were put into a trance sequence. Do you remember any of it?"

"Not much. Shadows. The memories are vague." I closed my eyes. I remembered holding a woman down, her cries of pleasure, the powerful thrust of my hips as the beast took what belonged to him.

"Shadows? That's why your cock is harder than my ion pistol?" the commander commented.

"Most males do not recall much of the processing data. Their higher levels of aggression during a ritual mating tend to obscure the experience."

I tried to process what he wasn't saying. "And the women? They go through the same process?"

He nodded enthusiastically as he removed a sensor from my temple. "Oh, yes. But the brides tend to recall everything." He cleared his throat. "Down to the most minute sensory detail."

Commander Deek laughed. "So, the males rut and walk away, and the females remember every detail forever so they can hold it against us later." He slapped me on the shoulder, hard. "Sounds about right for a mate."

"It is a consistent result of the testing," the man commented, "not a judgment on females in general."

I closed my eyes and sighed, ignoring the throbbing pulse of lust in my cock. If I saw my mate right now, and knew she was mine, I'd leap off this table, rip her clothing from her body, and impale her as I trapped her beneath me on this hard floor until she had so many orgasms that she begged me stop.

I envisioned her perfect, naked ass, pussy glistening with my come as she crawled away from me, her soft, round thighs pale in comparison to the soothing dark green of the medical bay floor. I'd let her crawl a bit, let her think I was finished with her, then grab her, flip her onto her back, throw her legs over my shoulders and fuck her again, my thumb on her clit as I made her chant my name. To anyone not of Atlan, it would sound barbaric, but we gave our mates what they needed, and they needed to know who they belonged to.

My cock pulsed and I growled, eager to find her, to fuck her. Now that I knew she was out there, ready for me, the beast tugged even harder to be free, to take what was his.

I was closer to the edge than I realized. With a supreme act of will, I reined in my need and focused on the conversation flowing around me as the medical officer spoke to Commander Deek.

"...it is often a sign of... compatibility before the bride's transport begins."

"Begin the transport then," I growled. "I am ready."

The doctor's assistant jumped and went to work at a wall screen near my feet, his gaze darting frantically from one item to another as his fingers flew over the controls. "Oh, um... yes. Well."

I tilted my head and looked up at him. He was a large warrior, not the size of an Atlan or Prillon fighter, but not small either. He'd been overly talkative, as most medical crew tended to be, but he wasn't just chatting now, he was flustered for some reason. Here I was, strapped to this table, torn between the need to fuck my mate and rip another Hive soldier to pieces, as he fumbled with the controls as if he'd never used them before. His ineptitude did not make it easier for me to maintain control.

"Let me get the doctor." The man dashed off before either of us could question him. In seconds, he was back with the small female doctor, her lush curves emphasized by the standard dark green instead of the assistant's gray. But I was too far gone to respect her knowledge or experience, or the fact that she very likely outranked me. I saw only a woman who needed fucking.

"I am Doctor Rone. I have just been told that while your match has been made, there is a slight complication."

My hands curled into fists and I fought against the tight restraints as the beast within raged, unhappy with this news. "What is the complication?" My voice was clipped and sharp.

The doctor cleared her throat and looked down at a data stream flowing across the portable tablet she carried. "Warlord Dax, your matched mate is a human woman from a planet called Earth. Her name is Sarah Mills. She is twenty-seven years of age, fertile, and meets all coalition bride processing requirements, but one."

Sarah Mills. Sarah Mills was mine. I looked at the back side of the tablet, eager for a look at my mate. "I would see her likeness."

The doctor shrugged, as if it made no difference to her, and held out the tablet so that I could see the dark-haired beauty staring out from the data screen. She was stunning and elegant, with delicate lines, arched brows, and a strong jaw more refined than any Atlan female's. Her long dark hair curved in waves and came to rest just below her shoulders. Her pink mouth looked ripe for kissing… or fucking. My hard cock jumped as I imagined her taking me in her mouth. I nearly came right there on the exam table. The sight of her intense, dark eyes made my mating fever so much harder to control. She was mine, and I wanted her now. Right fucking now. "Where is she?"

The doctor averted her gaze and stepped back, the tablet held protectively against her waist as she looked at Commander Deek for permission to speak.

What the fuck was going on with my mate?

"Where. Is. She?" I bellowed the question and all eyes in the medical station turned with curiosity in our direction. I tensed as the male Prillon doctor stepped in our direction, prepared to fight my way out of here if necessary. My little female doctor waved him off, apparently confident I wouldn't cause harm even though I was ready to rip this ship apart if the doctor didn't answer me.

Commander Deek rubbed his eyes and shook his head. We both knew this wasn't going to be good. "You'd better just tell us, doc."

The small female doctor remained composed, which was remarkable since my anger and frustration were setting off alarms across an entire wall of biological monitoring equipment. "I'm afraid she was reassigned—to a combat unit."

CHAPTER THREE

Dax

"Reassigned?" What? How did a matched mate become something else? The matching protocols used were precise and had been routine for hundreds of years. Once a match was made, there was no changing it unless the female found her mate unacceptable and asked for another. Even then, the psychological profile used by the process guaranteed the bride would be assigned a mate from the same planet.

"How can that be possible?" Commander Deek asked.

"Your match was made with an Earth woman." The doctor resumed her matter-of-fact perusal of the tablet data and ran her fingers over it a few times before looking at me again. "When she was processed for a match, you were not yet in the system. And since Earth allows their women to serve in combat positions, she elected to be reassigned to an active duty combat unit."

"What does that mean, exactly?" I was afraid I already knew the answer and could feel my rage building. What type of idiots allowed their weak, soft, helpless females to fight? "Where is she?"

The doctor's eyes filled with pity and the beast raged.

"She's in Sector 437, in command of her own recon unit assigned to the Battlegroup Karter."

"My *mate* refused me to go to the front lines and fight the Hive?"

My bellow shook the chair beneath me and I knew if I didn't calm down, right now, I'd tear this entire medical station to pieces and be one step closer to execution. Sector 437 was a known hotbed of Hive activity, and had been for the last eighteen months. This meant every second I sat in this damn chair my mate was in danger. The restraints weren't helping the monster within see reason. I'd expected my mate to be reassigned to a strategic unit, or perhaps one of the guardian ships that accompanied civilian cruisers through relatively safe flight zones. Not to be in active combat, engaging the enemy face to face! Not in one of the most dangerous sectors in the entire coalition front.

Calmer now, I repeated my question with a low growl. "She refused me?"

How dare an alien from Earth deny me and risk her life? Didn't she know that she was matched to an Atlan warlord? Being mine was an honor many elite Atlan females would fight over. And yet, this Earth female refused me?

"She didn't refuse you personally. She didn't know who her match was. In fact, she was processed several months ago. There was apparently some confusion on the part of bride processing center on Earth. It turns out she had never actually given her consent to be a bride, so she was allowed to opt out of the program and transfer to be a coalition fighter."

I saw red. The anger pulsed through my blood with hot fury. A bellow ripped from my lungs and I tensed, tugging with ease at the restraints and breaking through them. The doctor and her assistant both jumped back and everyone in the room began to scramble.

"Hell, Dax. You need to calm down. Calm down!" Commander Deek shouted.

I stood now, tugged at the wires still connected at my

temples and clenched my fists. I was breathing hard, as if I'd fought an entire brigade of Hive.

"Find another match." Commander Deek held his hand out in my direction, his size and my respect for him the only two things keeping me in place as the doctor shook her head.

"I can't. It doesn't work like that. I don't know why she wasn't removed from the system when she was transferred to the battle group. I'm not part of the bride processing unit. I don't have the authority or the ability to cancel a match or reassign a bride. We receive brides here; we don't process them. I will have to request a formal investigation of the events that occurred to create this complication during her processing on Earth."

The doctor crossed her arms and glared right back at me, as if seeing an Atlan warrior in battle rage in her medical station was not an unusual occurrence. Either that, or the woman was too brave for her own good. As I looked more closely, I realized the doctor did not look dissimilar from my mate.

"You look like her. Like my mate."

The doctor held out her hand. "Melissa Rone, from New York." When I simply stared at her outstretched hand, she dropped it to her side. "I'm from Earth as well. My primary mate is a Prillon captain."

I wanted to rip the heads from every living person in the room, and she offered her hand to me? Was she reckless or stupid, this human female with long dark hair and dark eyes, similar to my mate's? "Do you know my mate?"

"No. I'm from New York, she's from Miami. My dad was from Korea, and she looks like she has Greek, or maybe Italian heritage. We grew up on the same continent, though."

"That means nothing to me."

"Find him another match. He can't wait two years for her military service to be up."

I had all but forgotten Commander Deek as I studied the

woman, but he stood at my shoulder now, two Atlan warriors towering over a small, curvy female. She thinned her lips and I knew I was not going to like what she had to say.

"There is no other match. She is the only match for him. The system will not provide another compatible alternative unless she first accepts your match, goes through the thirty-day trial period, and requests a new mate. Or, she's deleted from the system."

Deleted meant dead. Killed in combat.

The doctor smiled and a knowing look entered her eyes. "Although, if you can get your hands on her, I imagine she won't want to leave you once the thirty days are up."

I imagined her shared by her two Prillon warriors, begging them to take her, and I smiled back. Perhaps a human woman could handle me after all, if my mate were as feisty an alien as this one. I needed to find my mate. I needed to fuck her. I wanted her now, with a sassy smile on her face and a wet pussy ready for me.

The doctor continued, "I could run the test a thousand times, but the results would be identical. The system will provide the exact same result. She is your only match."

My commander's hand held me back from breaking things. "Doctor Rone, this Atlan obviously has the mating fever upon him and there is no time for him to travel to the home planet to find an alternate."

My body was vibrating with the need to destroy something, to punch something, and the doctor studied me with an intensity and intelligence in her eyes I found disconcerting, as if she could see into my soul. Commander Deek continued when she remained silent.

"He needs his mate to soothe the fever, to ease the obvious... intensity of it. Transport him to her location immediately. He must claim her, or he *will* die."

The doctor looked at me, then the commander. "It is against protocol to transport an Atlan warrior with mating fever to another battle group. You could wipe out an entire squad before they killed you."

I growled deep in my chest and took a step toward her. "Send me to her now. She is *mine*."

The doctor actually chuckled. "No, she's not. She belongs to the Battlegroup Karter for the next…" she looked down at her tablet quickly then back up to meet my gaze, "…twenty-one months."

Commander Deek stepped in front of me and pushed me back, once, then twice. He was as big as I was, hulking over the doctor. He was also one of the only ones I'd allow to shove me without killing them, especially now when I fought the murderous rage that knowing my mate was in danger roused.

"There is an alternative, a loophole you could use to claim her."

He snarled at the woman over his shoulder. "Stop torturing the man and tell him what to do."

She nodded. "Big, growly males don't scare me, Commander Deek." She raised a brow as if for emphasis before putting me out of my misery. "Per coalition regulations, if she agrees to become your mate, she can request a transfer back to the bride program immediately. She would be released from all military obligations at once."

Finally, the female talked sense. My mating fever could be used to terminate my military service, if I chose to follow Atlan tradition. For my mate, volunteering for the bride program would do the same.

"Good. Send me to her. Now."

I wasn't happy with this turn of events, but I could still claim my mate. The way I felt, it would not be a hardship to travel to her sector and kill some Hive while I retrieved my mate. Then I'd punish her for putting herself in danger.

"Do you have her exact coordinates?" I asked, staring at the doctor over my commander's shoulder. I wondered if she would lie to me, relieved when she did not.

"I do."

All coalition citizens were tracked at all times.

"Transport me there. Now."

"You'll need your cuffs." The medical assistant came over and held out the cuffs for me, then changed his mind and gave them to the doctor before scurrying away. These were the mating cuffs, the last thing I wanted to wear. Besides being an outward—and obvious—sign that an Atlan was mated, it helped the Atlan males build their mating bond by ensuring close contact with their chosen female. Once I got the cuffs on her wrists, she wouldn't be able to go more than a hundred paces from my side until the fever was ended.

Up until an hour ago, I'd dreaded the stupid things, never interested in being mated myself or controlled in any way by the cuffs' technology. Now, everything had changed. Had they done something to me when I'd been asleep? Why did I now desperately need to go and find the one female who was matched to me, pull her from harm's way, and then turn her ass a fiery shade of red so she knew who was in charge of her safety... and so many other things?

I reached out and grabbed the cuffs, putting them on myself. They were a thick band of gold from the deepest mines on Atlan and had a thin strip of sensors on the insides that remained in contact with my body. They constantly monitored my physical health as well as provided a means of communication with the Atlan systems necessary for transport, purchasing goods, transfer of titles, and every other aspect of mated life, if I chose to continue to wear them after the fever was alleviated. More important, they offered some level of relief from the mating fever, for putting the cuffs about my wrist was proof that I had a chosen female. I was probably the only Atlan in the history of our world who had to hunt down his mate where she fought the Hive on the front lines.

She would be a legend before we even reached the home world. Our females did not fight. Ever.

That made me wonder. What kind of female was I about to be tangled with? The idea of a warrior bride should have made me cringe; instead I imagined her in the heat of battle with fire in her eyes and a female cry of rage that would closely mimic the sound she would make as I made her scream her pleasure while riding my cock. I wanted that fearless fire, that fury, directed at me so I could hold her down and let her buck and writhe and beg for release.

Fuck. My cock was hard as a rock and not at all comfortable stuffed inside my armor.

I closed one cuff around my left wrist, then the right, the seal on them secure. The match had been made, my mate identified. There was no going back. I would fight until I couldn't fight any longer, then take my mate home. I would grow old and fat on Atlan with a beautiful and well-fucked woman at my side. I felt the snugness of the bands, felt the weight and finality of my decision and let it settle around my shoulders like a cloak. I took a deep breath, then another, and grunted once the cuffs were secure.

The doctor held out a matching set of smaller cuffs meant for my bride and I clipped them onto the belt at my waist. She'd don them and be free from the military immediately. To her commander, it was a blatant sign of her mated status, a symbol that she belonged to me. While simply taking her wouldn't form a permanent bond—only fucking while the beast within was unleashed, with both sets of cuffs on our wrists would do that—the knowledge that she waited for me, that she needed me, that she could be under fire this very moment, made me impatient to claim her.

"Send me now, before I tear this ship apart."

My mate was in constant danger as a fighter. I stalked over to the transport pad located in the far corner of the medical station and cracked my neck side to side as I waited for one of the transport officers to communicate coordinates with the main system transporters. Normally, nothing but biological mass was allowed through the transport system, but when transporting onto the front lines, everything went for safety purposes. Armor and weapons included. I patted the ion pistol at my side and checked the knife on the other. All good.

"Good luck, Dax."

"I'll be back." I met Commander Deek's surprised look then tilted my head in the doctor's direction. "I see no reason to go home. Once my mate is secure and the fever is gone, I will settle onboard the Battleship Brekk with her and continue fighting, as the Prillon warriors do."

An Atlan female would never consent to that life, a life surrounded by war, but I was not ready to stop fighting the Hive, and my mate wouldn't be given the choice. She would be reassigned to caring for the children, or some other safe duty with the other women in the battle group. And me? I would fuck her every night and kill Hive every day. It would be perfect, as soon as I found her and fucked her into submission, fucked away the mating fever that boiled through my blood.

• • • • • • •

Sarah Mills, Sector 437, Recon Unit 7—Recovery of Freighter 927-4 from Hive scout teams

I stared down the scope of my ion rifle and watched as nine Hive scouts moved around the supply room with robotic precision. The Hive had invaded and taken over the coalition freighter two hours earlier, the crew's distress call still played in my mind like a broken record. The small ship's pilot had died screaming as I listened in the debriefing room. The eight coalition soldiers assigned to this small freighter were all either dead or transported to an integration station on a Hive outpost. We couldn't save them, but we could keep the Hive from acquiring the weapon stockpiles and raw materials in this hold.

Lifting my eye from my ion pistol's scope focused on the upper deck of the supply room, I motioned with two fingers for my team of twelve to split in three and move silently around the perimeter so we could surround them from above and pick them off like flies. We'd done this a dozen times in the last month and my unit moved like ghosts along the upper rigging in the room, their blasters at the ready.

It took a month of induction training to be ready to fight the Hive. All coalition recruits Earth sent to the battle battalions were required to have previous military experience—Earth military. It didn't matter which country a person fought for, only that they had extensive training in tactical, physical, and other skills they would need to fight the Hive. There were no homemakers or car wash attendees in the coalition fleet. That reassured me, for I'd been in the Army for eight years. I didn't need to be shot in the ass by a green recruit. Nor did I need to get killed because some inexperienced kid panicked at the sight of the silver cyborg soldiers.

The Hive made the old *Terminator* movies seem like bad 1950s sci-fi movies. Those cyborgs were slow to respond and more machine than human.

The Hive were much worse; streamlined and fast, they didn't wear clunky metal chunks and stomp around in moon boots made of iron. No, they were quick, highly intelligent, and, if they had civilian clothes on, could pass for biological if one didn't notice the silvery hue to their skin and eyes.

Hive cyborgs created from captured Prillon warriors were the worst I'd seen; big, mean and nearly impossible to kill without taking multiple shots.

But we had those gigantic Prillon motherfuckers on our side, too. Thank God.

I watched silently as Recon Unit 4, my brother Seth's unit, sneaked around the perimeter on the lower level, mirroring our positioning to make sure none of the Hive could escape down the lower level corridors once we started taking them out from above. I recognized my brother's movements easily, despite the armor disguising him. I'd been sneaking around the woods with him since we were old enough to walk and I watched, heart in my throat as he got close, too close, to one of the Hive who appeared to be scanning the inventory.

Seth stopped moving, blending into the shadows behind the scout, and I let the breath I'd been holding leak from my lungs.

It had taken me eight weeks to find my brother. A month of that I'd been in training, our assignments based on former military experience. Earth's soldiers were sent to ships all across the galaxy to fight the Hive. For me, it didn't hurt that in addition to my military service, I'd had eighteen years of *training* from my brothers and father in the swamps of Florida. They'd taught me self-defense and other skills I'd never considered useful—not until I faced the Hive. I could shoot better than most. I could fight dirtier than the others. Hell, I could even fly better than others. I was also routinely underestimated by both the coalition troops and the Hive. As I was the only woman in my recon unit, the men had thought I would crumble and cry in fear, but I'd more than held my own.

Hell, when I finally made it to the front lines—had it been four weeks ago?—three of my fellow new recruits had nervous breakdowns and had to be sent home before we saw our first fight. Taking on the Hive was *nothing* like what any of us had experienced on Earth and six recruits from my first unit had been killed in their first skirmish. Half the team. Dead.

None of my men questioned me now, for not only had I saved the other five with my marksmanship alone, we'd taken back that freighter from twelve Hive scouts and saved the ship and I'd flown the team home. Well, what was left of them. My analysis and battle strategies had made the commanding officers take notice. I'd been promoted my second day and was now in command of my own team, as was my brother. Unit 7 and Unit 4. Sarah and Seth. We took every assignment together we could, mostly because Seth and I each wanted to keep tabs on the other.

I held my dark, gloved fist up in the air, hand closed as

the last of my men moved into place. When I opened my fist, I'd begin a countdown from five that would signal the start of our attack. If things went well, it would be over in less than a minute.

If not—well, I preferred not to think about that.

Seth lifted his own fist, mirroring me to his team who were out of my line of sight.

We were ready.

Small squadrons like ours were made up almost entirely of humans from Earth. We were small, mean, and could get into tight places the hulking Prillon, Atlan, and other larger warriors could not. We humans were also more fragile and not as able to survive ground combat on some of the more hostile planet surfaces. I was perfectly happy to sneak around killing Hive in tight quarters rather than facing down seven- or eight-foot-tall giants on the ground.

No, humans, for the most part, were placed in recon units; small, strategic forces inserted into high-risk zones near a battle where we could either merge with other units to form a larger fighting group, usually behind enemy lines, or missions like this where we sneaked in and took back what was ours.

My brother's eyes met mine and he gifted me with a broad smile. My heart shifted with a painful twist in my chest. I'd missed him. His dark hair, the same shade as mine, was cut military short. While I'd gotten my father's height, Seth was half a head taller than me. He looked fit, well rested. Besides the tension of battle on his face, the constant awareness of his surroundings honed by the military, he looked exactly the same as he had the day he'd volunteered for the battle battalion with Chris and John.

I'd found him. I'd done it. I'd fulfilled my deathbed promise to my father and found Seth. While I couldn't take him back to Earth—both of us still had time left on our terms of service—I could stay near him, even fight beside him as I did today.

A loud blast sounded over our heads and I dropped to

the floor and looked at the three soldiers hidden with me to see if they knew what was going on. They all stared back at me with blank, shocked expressions but maintained radio silence.

What the hell was that?

The Hive were running and shots were fired down below. Radio silence was broken as Seth issued orders. "Fire! Fire!"

The hissing sound of ion blasters filled the air along with cries of pain as some of our men went down. The screen inside my helmet listed off two of my men as casualties.

Shit. Shit. Shit! All hell was breaking loose.

"Mitchell and Banks are down on the left. You two, go around to the left flank." I pointed in the direction I wanted two of my soldiers to go. "Get them out of there."

They took off and I turned to Richards, my right-hand man. "Head right but don't start shooting until I give you cover fire. Find out what the hell just dropped in on us."

"Yes, sir."

Richards took off in a low crouching run and I lifted my head above the galley railing to try to figure out what was going on.

"Report. Everybody. Talk to me. What the hell is going on?" I checked my weapons as my team checked in. An unauthorized transport had occurred.

"Seth?"

My brother's voice came through the clear. "Some big motherfucker just dropped in on top of us without warning. I think he's ours, but it set off the Hive and they've got six more scouts down here. I've got three men down at three o'clock."

I peeked over the railing, beyond furious that the coalition had transported someone in without warning us. My brother was right, he was *huge*. And completely insane. As I watched, he pulled the head off the Hive scout closest to him with his bare hands, completely ignoring an ion blast from one of the smaller Hive weapons.

Holy shit. I'd never seen *anything* like that before.

The giant's bellow echoed like a cannon blast in the small space and I winced.

"At least he appears to be on our side." Was that sarcastic voice really mine? I'd just watched a giant alien rip off another alien's head with his bare hands, and I was cracking jokes? My dad would be so damn proud.

"Roger that." Seth sounded like he was amused as well. "He's an Atlan."

Wow. I'd heard of them, but never seen one in action. They were generally ground troops, huge, strong, fast, and brutally efficient killers. With Gigantor on our side, it was time to switch tactics. "Recon 7, shoot to kill, but try not to hit the giant. Let's finish this."

"Yes, sir."

Ion blaster fire was so thick I could barely see what was happening as I rose from my hidden position and opened fire. I took out two scouts, the giant took out three more, and the rest of our teams took out the remaining few. We all wore our tactical gear—lightweight, basic black and brown armor that would shield a low-level ion blast. It wasn't pretty, but I thought of it as space camo. Our helmets filtered the air and provided constant levels of oxygen and pressure optimized to our species. Our ion pistols were lightweight and computer assisted, but metallic armor could deflect a blast. Strapped to our thighs were two things we never left without: a blade—for close combat and things that got up close and personal—and a very human injector filled with a lethal dose of poison.

The injector was a personal choice offered to all soldiers who volunteered from Earth. The suicide injection was an option both Seth and I carried gladly. I'd seen what happened to soldiers who were taken by the Hive, and death was preferable to losing myself in their Hive mind, turned into something less than human. I didn't know if other worlds offered their warriors that out, nor did I care. No one wanted to be taken by the Hive alive. I'd been told the injector was filled with the most deadly poison known to the coalition. There was no antidote, and death was certain within a few seconds.

Anything was better than ending up one of those silver-eyed automatons. One thing we'd learned quickly enough was that the Hive didn't have any sense of honor. They rarely killed, preferring to take prisoners to their integration centers where they would implant Hive technology into the biologicals until they were no longer in control of their own bodies. They became one with the Hive. A drone. For all intents and purposes, a walking computer that followed orders from the Hive mind.

The Hive were merciless fighters and we had to focus on that. Do our jobs—remove the Hive from this freighter and get the hell out, transported back to base, a hot dinner, and sleep before another mission. Live to fight another day. *That* was the goal.

Not only did I have to keep my men alive, but my brother, too.

The sounds of ion blasts died down, the bright flares of weapon fire fading away. Fortunately for us, the freighter was full of supplies as rows upon rows of crates filled the cavernous cargo area, affording us a good deal of protection. Unfortunately, this meant the Hive had cover as well.

We'd meant to take them by surprise, corral the Hive into the center, forcing them into a smaller and smaller space, like an anaconda squeezing the life out of its prey. But the Atlan warrior had ruined our plans, crashed our party, and not in a good way. Fuming, I took stock. I had two men down, but the Hive appeared to be routed.

"Recon 7, report."

I listened to my men as they checked in.

"Six is clear."

"Three is clear. Two men down."

I sighed, but let it go. Shit happened. Soldiers died. I'd think about it later, when I was writing letters to their families and crying my eyes out. *Later.* "Richards?"

"Nine is clear."

I waited, expecting to hear from Seth, who was at the twelve o'clock position on the lower deck.

"Recon 4?"

I heard Seth's voice, loud and clear. "You better get down here."

I ordered my men to remain on the high ground and ran down the ramp to my brother. It wasn't just the Hive that had my eyes widening as I approached.

"Holy shit," I whispered.

It was this… this warrior who had transported in. He wore the coalition uniform, but it fit him in a way that had my mouth falling open. He wore no helmet, his face rugged but not what I would have expected from an alien. He looked almost human, just a lot bigger. There could have been ion blasts zinging over my head, but I wouldn't have noticed. He was definitely tall—easily pushing seven foot, dark and handsome, but the size of a lumberjack. A bloody lumberjack, for he was covered in Hive blood, from a pile of dead, decapitated bodies that lay strewn about his feet like trash. He hadn't even pulled his blaster free from its holster at his side. His arms had to be as thick as my thighs, and I was no waif. He made my heart skip a beat and my breathing catch in a way not even a Hive fight could muster.

He stood tall and confident, perhaps too confident, for he ignored the destruction around him and searched… for something. Or someone. Even from a distance, I heard his low growling and saw his entire body strung up tight as a bow, ready to take the head of the next idiot stupid enough to gain his attention. His dark eyes had an intensity unlike any I'd ever seen. I gulped when they were turned my way. I ignored him, thinking that it was because I didn't want to have my head torn off. In fact, I didn't want all that intensity focused on me.

CHAPTER FOUR

Sarah

With all the ion blasts that had been crisscrossing the area during the skirmish, he should have ducked, even pulled his own ion pistol from his hip, but he hadn't. He scanned left, then right as I heard an all too familiar buzzing sound from the side.

Three more Hive transported into the room just a few steps from me and attacked. Seeing that one of the new Hive was going to shoot me, the Atlan didn't even blink. I swear he grew in size, as if he'd been inflated like a balloon. He was angry. Furious even, for the tendons in his neck stood out and his jaw clenched. His eyes narrowed and he grabbed the Hive warrior and literally ripped his head off without even drawing his ion pistol. Blood spurted everywhere as he threw the body at his comrades before charging them.

I should have tried to help, but I rolled to the side and came up on my knee, rifle at the ready.

Too late, the three were already dead. More bodies at his feet like sacrifices to a bloodthirsty god.

I stared, shocked at the carnage. Two of Seth's men

came up to flank me, staring like I was. I was quite sure none of us had ever seen anything this brutal, on Earth or anywhere else. I had no idea why the alien was even carrying a weapon. Those hands, those huge hands, were weapons themselves. I knew it was an Earth saying that when someone was mad they'd rip your head off, but this... shit, this was the real deal.

Seth chuckled in my ear and stepped out from behind a cargo container as I stayed on my knee, my rifle now pointed at the alien growling like a bear.

"Welcome to our little raiding party, Atlan. I'm Captain Mills." Seth didn't raise his rifle, but he didn't put it away either. I held mine steady, pointed at the warrior's head.

The giant grunted and stood to his full height, which made me blink. Hard. His shoulders were massive, his chest big enough for a big girl like me to curl up against. I wanted to *touch*, and the urge was annoying. When the giant spoke, his deep, rumbly voice traveled straight to my core, my nipples growing hard. Sex on a stick. Good God, he was the hottest man I'd ever seen. Ever.

"You are not Captain Sarah Mills."

Seth laughed and I felt my heart skip a beat. *Captain Sarah Mills?* This warrior knew who I was?

Choosing to remain silent, I met my brother's gaze for a heartbeat of time and nodded for him to continue. If this big guy was looking for me, I wasn't sure I wanted to be found.

Seth took off his helmet and held it under his left arm, his right still holding his ion blaster. "No, I'm not. That would be my sister, who got lucky on her ASVAB and learned how to fly. What do you want with Captain Mills?"

Instead of answering, the warrior clenched his fists at his sides as if fighting for control. All around me rifles were held steady as we waited to see what the Atlan was going to do. "She is not here?"

"Who's asking?" Seth raised his ion blaster to make sure the Atlan knew to be on his best behavior. "I don't know

41

you, soldier. You transported into a live op, and endangered two units. I've got five dead because you blew our surprise. From where I'm standing, I should shoot your ass and get on with cleaning up your mess."

The Atlan slumped, as if bothered by what my brother said. "I apologize for your loss. We did not realize I would be transporting into an active combat zone. It was a terrible mistake."

"Why are you here?"

I tightened by grip on my rifle waiting for his answer.

"I am looking for Captain Sarah Mills."

"Why?"

"She's mine."

My head was shaking a *hell, no* before I had even processed his words. Eyebrows raised, I stood and lowered my rifle. "Seven, keep him in your sights."

A chorus of acknowledgments sounded in my ears as I lowered my ion blaster and tried to decide what to do. The giant turned at the sound of my voice and I removed my helmet, dropping it to the floor. He looked as if he would move toward me, and I raised my blaster to stop him. "Don't."

"You are Sarah Mills."

"How do you know me? I don't know any Atlans." Meeting his gaze was a huge mistake as the instant lust I'd felt watching him earlier returned full force. I was tempted to lick my lips and tease him closer, which was just stupid. As I stared with as blank an expression as I could manage, a strange buzz danced over the skin of my neck and face. I tensed, my gaze flying to Seth. His eyes widened as he felt the energy building.

"Incoming!" I shouted, diving for the floor as a blast of energy cleared the center of the room.

When the concussion ended, three Hive soldiers stood in the exact spot we'd fled.

The Atlan roared, charging. My men opened fire from the upper decks at the surprise Hive. The soldiers did not attack as I feared, but nodded to each other and disappeared—transported into thin air—one by one.

The last, however, was inches from Seth. He grabbed my brother and spun, hoisting Seth into the air to use as a human shield as my brother's ion rifle clattered to the floor at his feet.

Seth!

I lifted my pistol, but I couldn't take a shot without hitting my brother. The Atlan looked at them and froze mid-stride. All my training kept me in position, my aim steady as we waited to see what the Hive soldier would do.

"Release him." I yelled at the Hive soldier, but he ignored me, his gaze on the real threat, the Atlan giant just a few paces away.

Seth kicked, reaching for the injector at his side as he screamed at all of us. "Do it! Take him out."

"No!" I screamed at my brother as the Hive stepped back, further away from us, my brother held to his chest like a shield.

In my ear, Richards' voice was like the devil's own temptation. "I can take the shot, captain." He was above me, and a decent shot, but not perfect, nowhere close to a true marksman, and this was my brother's life on the line. Richards would have about a four-inch window to kill the Hive soldier and leave Seth breathing.

"No. Not yet."

The Hive warrior holding Seth lifted his weapon and aimed it at the Atlan. We were all frozen as the emotionless silver eyes of the Hive soldier scanned the room. Before we could do more, the Hive pressed a button on his uniform and he… he disappeared. So did Seth.

Gone. Poof. Into thin air. On Earth there was no such thing as transporting. It was something for old TV shows, but never in real life. Only those fighting with the coalition saw it in real life. *Beam me up, Scotty.* The first time I'd been transported, I'd been terrified. The technology was supposed to be cool and had been, until now. Now, my brother had been transported somewhere, somewhere Hive. Somewhere I knew they turned coalition fighters into machines, replacing body parts with synthetic implants until there was nothing of the individual left. He was there one second, gone the next.

Unless my brother chose door number two. All at once the memory of his hand reaching for the injector at his thigh played like a broken record in my mind. "Seth!" I screamed.

The crazy Atlan—the one who'd wrecked our op and caused the Hive to take my brother—turned his head and stared at me. Those dark eyes narrowed, his full lips thinning. He wouldn't look away, not even when every ion blaster in the room was pointed in his direction. I felt something, something primeval and explosive flare to life in me as our gazes locked.

Holy hell. He was... and I felt... and... shit. My brain was misfiring. My body disregarding any notion of personal safety as I marched up to the man, ready to attack with every ounce of strength I had left. I raised my ion pistol and advanced until I had the business end pressed into the warrior's armor, right over his heart. I stared up into those eyes and realized he hadn't tried to stop me. He hadn't touched me at all, instead his dark gaze filled with pain as he looked upon me.

Our gazes held and I couldn't do it, couldn't pull the trigger. I studied his hard jaw and full mouth, the dark eyes and the black, silken hair that fell to his chin. He was truly stunning to the senses, his strength staggering and overwhelming. Even with the rage pulsing through my body, I couldn't pull the trigger. My brother's capture wasn't truly this warrior's fault. It was no one's fault. It was war. And war sucked.

"Captain!" Richards' voice broke me from my trance and I lowered the weapon, but didn't back away from the warrior.

"You will help me recover my brother."

His eyes widened in surprise, but he nodded. "You have

my word." That voice, those four words, were like a rockslide. Harsh, rough, and deep.

Mollified for the moment, I took a step back.

"Coalition clear!" I shouted, signaling it was safe to stand. It was time to get the hell out of here.

The Atlan watched me closely, but didn't move. We all knew by his uniform that he was coalition, but the way he'd behaved, the blood coating his hands? He was a threat and his silence helped us all calm down and not kill him.

"I want four of you to remain here and watch our back. Three Hive transported in and took Captain Mills," I said, irate that they'd been able to infiltrate and take Seth. *He'd* let it happen. "And you."

I pointed at the rogue fighter.

His gaze swept the room, then met mine. There was heat when he looked at me, desire. And that pissed me off. We were in the middle of a war zone. I didn't need—or want to be—attracted to anyone in the middle of a battle. I was no skinny thing, but his gaze made me feel small and feminine. Feminine? That was crazy because I was anything but in my coalition body armor. The curve of my breasts was well hidden behind the chest armor. My hips were disguised under the black armored pants. No one else here saw me as a woman. I was their leader and that was all.

The fact that he'd made me think about sex right now caused my muscles to go rigid with fury.

"Who the hell are you and why are you looking for me?" I demanded.

"I am Warlord Dax from Atlan and I am your matched mate. You are mine."

"Are you kidding me with this? Is this the mouse's idea of a joke? I'm not a bride, Warlord Dax from Atlan. Sorry. You'll just have to fuck off." I threw my hands in the air and nodded to Seth's team. With Seth gone, they were mine now. My responsibility. "Four of you stay here, stay sharp. Set up a transport block so we don't get any more surprises."

"Yes, sir."

"Medics, secure the wounded, make sure we've done everything we can and get them transported out." I walked toward the door. "Three of you with me to the bridge. Richards, I want you on system checks. My unit, grab someone from four and check the other decks. You guys know the drill."

Both teams scurried to do as ordered and I ignored the big alien as he fell into step beside me. I felt like a cocker spaniel walking next to a Rottweiler. Still, we had three armed members of my unit at our backs, and I was still carrying my ion pistol.

"This term you use, fuck? It is associated solely with a man rutting a woman and bringing her pleasure, not with... battle."

The men about me relaxed a little at his words, thinking Dax was joking. He wasn't. Heat flared to my cheeks, but it wasn't out of embarrassment. No, it was the instant mental picture of this warlord pressing me up against the nearest wall, ripping my pants open and rutting into me.

If I ever went back to Earth, I was going to murder a certain mouse.

"What is your problem?" It felt much better to divert my interest in him into frustration. "Didn't they tell you I opted out of the bride program?"

"Yes."

I stopped in my tracks at his admission and he took a step closer so I had to tilt my chin up to meet his dark eyes. I wouldn't retreat. His gaze roved over my face, then lower down my body. It was not the look of any warrior I had ever worked with. This was blatant and sexual, full of a possessive heat I'd never seen before and... holy shit, my nipples just hardened. Thank God for the chest armor.

"Do you think that matters to me?" He arched a brow as if he expected me to bow my head and let him lead me away like a fairytale princess. That was so not happening. Nothing was happening until I got my men back onboard the Karter and my brother back from the Hive.

He reached out to grab my arm, but I lifted my ion pistol halting him, the hilt of it nudging his hard armor. My men also aimed their weapons on him. He paused, but didn't seem the least bothered... or afraid that he was going to die if he made one wrong move.

"Stand down," he commanded.

No one followed his order and I raised an eyebrow in silent pleasure, knowing my men would stand behind me.

"If my title of warlord isn't enough, the stripes on my uniform indicate that I outrank all of you," he said, pointing with a bloody finger to the symbol on his shoulder. "I am pleased to see you defend and protect my mate, but you will stand down or face military punishment."

He was correct. While he was clearly from a different planet, a planet where the men ate lots of spinach like Popeye to grow so big, he wore the coalition uniform we all recognized. He *was* a higher rank than me and we were, technically, required to obey his commands.

My men remained with their weapons raised and I realized this all hinged on me. If I told my men to fight the big, bad alien, they would. But they'd most likely end up in some coalition prison because I couldn't control my temper. I was not in the habit of asking my men to sacrifice themselves for me, especially for something this ridiculous.

Turning my head, I nodded at them to lower their weapons. This was a battle for Commander Karter's ears. It would have to wait until we got back to our battleship.

He looked at me and it was his turn to arch a brow, for I had yet to move my weapon from his belly. While he was now in charge of the group on the freighter, it didn't mean I wouldn't continue to be mad at him. Grudgingly, I lowered the weapon.

"What are you—do you have any idea what you did?" I clenched my hands into fists at my sides so I wouldn't hit him with them. "I lost good men today. And the Hive just took my brother!"

"I am sorry for your lost warriors. But your brother should have kept you safe on Earth, where you belong. A woman does not belong out here, in combat, fighting the enemy," he countered.

"My *brother* has no say in what I do."

"Obviously. *I*, however, do."

My eyes widened then and I laughed. "You might outrank me, *sir*," I placed a heavy influence on the last word, "but you are not my mate."

"With all due respect, warlord," my second-in-command, Shepard, moved to stand beside me. He seemed to give this... Dax more deference than I. But he wasn't being called the big guy's *mate*. "I have to question the... accuracy of your claim. Captain Mills has been with us for two months. Earth's laws don't allow a soldier to enter the battle battalion program if they are married. Or mated."

Shepard was diplomatic, clearly fearful to call this warlord an idiot. But Dax had to be wrong, absolutely wrong, for there was no way I was mated to this overbearing brute. Even my subconscious wouldn't be that cruel to me.

Instead of ripping Shepard's head off, Dax replied, "This Earth female is my chosen mate through the Interstellar Bride Program and I am claiming her."

Oh, shit. He *was* from Atlan. The planet Warden Egara said I'd be matched to. I shook my head. "I left the program because it was all a mistake. The warden said that I couldn't be matched if I didn't consent. I'm a soldier now, and I'm pretty sure there's nothing you can do about it."

"You will tell Commander Karter that you are my mate and resign your commission with the coalition fleet." He was clearly ignoring everything I was saying.

I placed my hands on my hips. "I will do no such thing, you big oaf."

He frowned. "I do not know that term, but mate will suffice."

I took a step back, not because I was afraid of Dax, but because he might actually be right about this stupid mess. I remembered that little idiot of an assistant, Warden Morda, and how she'd messed up everything to start with. Could she have done something else to screw up after I was inducted into the coalition fleet? Something like not delete my profile, not take me out of the system?

Oh, crap.

"We have been matched." He leaned forward, his gaze never breaking eye contact. "You are mine."

I shuddered. I couldn't be a mate. I certainly couldn't go after Seth if I was forced out of the military to become someone's bride. I doubted this huge hulk of an alien wanted me to do much of anything besides birth babies. He'd already said women didn't belong in combat. That didn't make me believe he would want me to take a team to a Hive integration center and save Seth.

Still, he'd already given me his word that he would help get my brother back.

More likely, he planned to pat me on the head like a good little girl and leave me behind while he went out to slay dragons. I got a very obvious overprotective vibe from him. And that was not my style.

Could he force me to resign my commission with the fleet? I didn't know the rules. Since I'd been matched by their system, could he force me out of the military? Could this giant Atlan male force my hand?

Besides that, I didn't *want* a mate. I'd had to deal with enough men in my life—a pesky father, three brothers, commanders in the military, fellow soldiers—I didn't need a mate, too. And him? *Him!* God, this man was matched to me? So far, he'd done nothing but piss me off. So what if he was sex on a stick—sex on a *very big* stick. So what if my mind conjured images of him fucking me up against a wall, pounding into me hard over and over until I came all over his very large cock? And I knew it was large. It had to be.

I refused to believe my feelings were caused by any kind of mating… thing. More likely, I took notice of him due to the epic sex drought I was in. Two and a half years without sex would drive any sane woman to take notice of the huge male. I just wanted an orgasm or two and I wasn't opposed to the idea of him giving them to me. Just because I was a woman didn't mean I couldn't fuck, then walk away. *Hit it and quit it* could work for me, too. Right?

This attraction was purely biological. He made my nipples hard, so what? Cold weather did the same thing and being from Florida, I hated snow, too. Dax was obviously bossy and blatantly chauvinistic and domineering and overwhelming… and on and on. I'd lucked out, choosing the coalition over him. Mated… to him! Ha!

"I'm not going with you, you're welcome to come with us," I told him, nudging him with the tip of my ion pistol. "Shepard, are we back in coalition space?"

Shepard checked his data pad and nodded. "Yes, sir."

"Excellent." My men would be safe now, the ship protected by coalition patrols and escorted back to the battle group for cleanup and reassignment. "Shep, you're in charge of cleanup. I'm taking my *mate*—" I said the word with disdain and sarcasm, "—back to the Karter. We have business to take care of."

Dax frowned down at me but I refused to look away. "*You* are coming with me to the Brekk."

I raised my pistol and narrowed my eyes. "No. I'm not. *We* are going to go find Commander Karter, plan a rescue mission, and get a space divorce."

I think he actually growled. What the hell? Was he part beast or something?

CHAPTER FIVE

Dax

It took an hour for my mate to debrief her commanding officer about the events of the battle I'd transported directly into. That done, we had been ordered to report to Commander Karter's war room on the command deck. Now we stood opposite Commander Karter's desk. My mate stood at attention beside me in front of the Prillon leader. Like all Prillon commanders, he was almost as big as I, with golden hair and eyes that stared at us both like the predator he was. There was no softness in his expression or empathy in his eyes. He sat stiff and at attention behind his desk, calculating and calm despite my mate's growing irritation.

"I want to go after him," she told her commander, her chin set at a defiant tilt. I stood, listening only. I bided my time, for my chance to speak would come soon. "I'll take volunteers."

Her commander sighed and continued to ignore me. "I can't sanction a rescue mission to an integration center for one coalition fighter. Things are precarious enough around here, captain, as it is. I can't risk warriors for a mission that is most likely doomed to failure. We're holding this sector by sheer force of will. I can't risk the lives of good, strong fighters on a suicide run for a man who is probably already lost."

And there it was, the truth my mate didn't want to hear. I could see the mix of fury and sadness flicker across her face, but she disguised it well. "I have to try. He's my brother."

Her pain made me ache to pull her to me and hold her close. The strength of the urge to hug an alien female, to soothe her emotions, only confirmed that I was at the mercy of the mating connection. I studied her now, at my leisure, as she stood before her commander and tried to hide her hurt with a fierce pride I admired. She looked so much more vibrant and beautiful than the image I'd seen on the doctor's tablet. That image had been flat, without her fire or the stubborn tilt of her jaw. In reality, she looked like so much... more.

She wore the familiar uniform of a coalition fighter, the body armor easily disguising every one of her curves. Perhaps it was because she was my mate, or because she was so damn attractive, but I wanted her with a ferocity I'd never experienced before. I had to focus to listen to her conversation with the commander as visions of ripping her armor to shreds and exploring her curves with my tongue nearly overwhelmed me. She was *all* woman, and she was mine. Her dark hair was pulled back in some kind of snug ball at the back of her neck. I had to wonder what it would feel like tangled in my fingers as I tugged her head back for a kiss. Her skin was pale, so much fairer than mine or anyone else's on Atlan. I doubted she reached more than my chin, but she was large for a female. She wasn't delicate or dainty, but obviously brash and bold and sassy as hell. My inner beast loved all that fire and my cock wanted to taste it. The beast in me clawed to come out, toss her over my shoulder, and carry her away.

I knew any man who looked at her would be instantly

attracted and I fought the primal urge to mark her with my scent, rub my skin and my seed all over her flesh to make sure every male who came close to her knew exactly who she belonged to. She was mine and I needed everyone to know it, including the stubborn female who, even now, was trying to figure out a way to rid herself of me. All I could think about was burying my cock inside her, and all she wanted was to force me to leave her side.

The challenge riled my beast in a way I had not anticipated, and I felt myself eager to taste her teeth and claws in the bedroom. How she'd ended up unmated until now was beyond me. How was it possible no male on Earth had desired her, or claimed her? It made me think that there was something wrong with that species of males. Human men must be idiots.

"I'm aware that he is your relation." Commander Karter held up his hand as she was about to speak again. "I'm also aware that two of your brothers already died at the hands of the Hive. I'm sorry for your loss, but there is nothing I can do."

Two brothers died at the hands of the Hive? That explained quite a bit. How many more brothers did she have? Were Earth families close like they were on Atlan? Was there a kinship, a love, between siblings that drove her need to rescue him? If this was the case, I understood, for I had one brother as well. If he were captured, I too would try to rescue him. But she was female and my mate. If she needed to know her brother was safe, I would take care of it for her.

I grumbled and both she and her commander turned to me.

"I will go after her brother. It was my interference that led to his capture."

I shouldn't be impressed by her warrior abilities, the tactical skill I'd witnessed on that freighter. Females didn't fight. They placated, soothed, nurtured. They weren't stupid; in fact, quite the opposite. A female was the only one who could tame her mate's inner beast and that took keen intelligence. The initial mating fever was depleted by the bonding, but the beast's unpredictable rage never truly went away. Our mates knew how to soothe the angst that raged within, often silently. I had never known such a level of anger and rage as when she was in grave danger.

I wanted to protect her, fuck her, care for her. But Sarah Mills didn't want a mate and she didn't seem like much of a soother. So, I would win her heart the only way I could, by getting her brother back for her.

The commander leaned back in his chair and crossed his arms over his massive chest. Were I human, I may have been intimidated, but I was Atlan, and even larger than the Prillon warrior glaring at me now. I welcomed his ire, happy to redirect his irritation away from my mate. "You are another problem entirely, Warlord Dax. What the hell are you doing in my sector without authorization?"

"I came for my mate."

"I'm a warrior, not a mate. I told the bride program that. I'm sorry you didn't get the memo." She looked at the commander. "Can you assign me to a squadron that is perhaps at least fighting in an area around their closest integration center?"

"Do you want to be captured and turned into a cyborg?" I asked, my voice loud in the small room. She refused to relent and I refused to leave without her. I couldn't. While the cuffs were not on her wrists—yet—I would not abandon my mate. She was mine and I would protect her— even from herself—with my life.

She rolled her eyes. "No, but I have to save my brother."

"No, you do not. I shall retrieve him for you."

She opened her mouth, her gaze spitting fire, but the commander rose from his seat and slammed his hand down on his desk. "Neither one of you is going into Hive territory to rescue a dead man. Captain Mills, your brother is dead. If they didn't kill him outright, he's been integrated into their Hive mind, his body altered with synthetic technology we will be unable to remove. He is dead. I'm sorry. The answer is no."

The commander turned to me. "And you, Warlord Dax, will get back to the transport room and leave my ship. From what I heard of your actions, I don't need you to go into berserker mode and be put down. Get to Atlan and find a new mate."

"My mate is here. If I leave this ship, she is coming with me."

Although it was true, I preferred my mate accept our match, forced bonding *was* possible. Sometimes, it was the only way to save a warrior's life. I would not force her to accept the bond, but simply being in her presence soothed my beast. I would seduce her, make her come over and over until she thought of nothing but pleasing me, fucking me, soothing me.

I crossed my arms over my chest. I knew she would not like to be commanded, but I would carry her off if necessary.

I didn't need a full bond to hold off the beast for now, I just needed to be near her. Forced bonding was dishonorable, a desperate act by a desperate man, and something I would not do. Forcing the link between us boded poorly for the union long term. If I was going to be mated with this Earth female for the remainder of our lives, I wanted her to at least like me. I wanted to fuck her, coddle her, cherish her—and fuck her some more, but I would not take an unwilling female.

I'd rather die.

However, seduction was a game I was eager to play.

"She isn't leaving with you, warlord, because she hasn't accepted your match. She's not a coalition bride, she's Captain Mills of Recon Unit 7." The commander was equally adamant. "Right now, she's mine. *Prillon* warriors do not force females into mating bonds they do not want."

Sarah grinned then and my cock swelled. There was no question she was even more lovely when she wasn't all stiff and proper. She felt victorious and powerful with the commander backing her, but that wasn't going to get her what she needed to be happy and it was time to remind her of that.

I pointed at the commander, but turned to face her. "He won't let you go get your brother."

Her gaze darted from my face to her commander. "What *can* I do?"

"Go back to your unit and follow orders until your two years is up." When her shoulders stiffened at the commander's direct words, he added. "You're one of the best recon leaders we have. You're smart, fast, and don't panic under fire. The men trust you. You could do a lot of good here, captain. We need officers like you."

I growled again; the thought of my mate going back into battle without me by her side was more than my beast could tolerate. Just thinking of the firefight I'd witnessed, ion blasts darting over her head, made my beast begin to pace. The commander would know my displeasure at his words. For a Prillon, he was big, but I was bigger. "She is *not* going back to battle."

"Go home to Atlan, warlord," he countered. "Find another mate."

"I want no other."

Sarah's shoulders tensed at my vow and her gaze darted to my face as if she did not believe my words.

"Then wait for her two years of service to be up," the commander ordered.

"Like hell," I growled. "I'll be dead by then."

Her eyebrows went up.

The commander looked me over. "Mating fever? How much time do you have?"

"Not much." I offered him the brief response while I stared at Sarah.

"What do you mean you'll be dead? You're sick?" she asked me. I saw concern fight for space in her heart, right next to her anger. Perhaps there was hope for us after all.

"Commander, may I please speak with my mate... in private?"

The Prillon glanced between the two of us. When Sarah nodded, he walked out without another word, the door sliding shut behind him.

Seeing her worry gave me some measure of hope.

"Mating fever," I told her. "Atlan males have it, although when it strikes is unique to each individual. It lasts for several weeks, slowly building until it is all consuming. I'm older than most who get the fever, but that is irrelevant. When it takes over, it overpowers logic and reasoning and turns the male—me—into what we call a berserker." I held up my stained hands. "My body transforms into more beast than man. Rage fills me until there is no reason left, only pure animal instinct. I can rip the heads off the Hive without blinking, but I won't want to stop. The only thing that can control an Atlan berserker is his mate. The only way to calm the beast is to be soothed and accepted by our mates, to fuck."

Her eyes widened.

"And if you don't... fuck, you die? That doesn't make sense." she said, surprised. Just hearing the word *fuck* from her lips made me groan.

"It is called *mating* fever for a reason. It is meant to ensure that all Atlan males are appropriately matched and mated, allowing for the continuation of the species. If a male doesn't mate, he dies."

"Like survival of the fittest," she replied.

"I do not know that term."

She held up her hand. "It doesn't matter, but I understand... the concept. If you have to fuck someone, then go find a space prostitute or something," she countered, waving a hand in the air. "You don't need me. Any vagina will do."

Anger swelled at her last statement. "Not anyone will do," I growled, then took a deep breath. Of course, a short while ago I'd thought differently, but now she was in front of me. Now I knew, deep down to my soul, that this Earth woman was mine. I didn't need a matching program for verification. "It's the *mating* fever. This means that it can only end by fucking a *mate*. In my case, this means you."

When she remained silent, I pushed on. Stepping closer, I said, "Do you know what I see when I look at you?"

She shook her head.

"The palest of skin I want to touch. I wonder how soft it is. Are you soft everywhere? Your breasts, you try to hide them beneath your body armor, but they are round and full. Easily a handful. I want to cup them and feel their weight. I want to watch as your nipples tighten when I stroke my thumbs over them. That plump lower lip, I wonder how it will feel when I nibble on it. And your pussy—"

She held up a hand, most likely to push me away, but her hand settled on my chest. I covered her hand with mine and walked her backward until she bumped into the wall. I didn't give her space—that wasn't what she needed—and I pressed one of my legs between hers. Because of the height difference, she practically rode my thigh.

I watched as her pupils dilated, her mouth fell open. Good, she wasn't thinking now. If there was a female who needed to stop thinking, it was this one. She needed someone else to watch out for her, to take care of her for a change. Starting right now.

"You are mine, Sarah, and I will not give you up."

"I have to fuck you and then you'll be cured? You won't die?" She looked me over in a very heated way and I let her look, let her see the desire in my eyes, feel the heat of my body close to hers. "Fine. I'll fuck you once—a one-night stand—and then we can go our own separate ways. It's been a while and I'm sure you're… probably… an interesting lover."

While I found her agreement appealing, I shook my head, for she still didn't understand. "There is no *own separate ways*. We mate for life. And, getting back to the mating fever, it's not just once. We will have to fuck again and again…" I leaned closer, nudging her cheek with my nose, breathing in her sweet scent, "...until the fever is soothed, until it has passed."

She lifted both hands to my chest and I grabbed her wrists, pinning them over her head as I continued my exploration of her neck, then buried my nose behind her ear to smell her hair. Her breathing became ragged as she whispered in my ear, "And if I won't fuck you again and again until the fever is soothed?"

"I die."

"You want me to be your mate so you don't die?" she asked. I lifted my head and looked her in the eye, our lips apart. My respect for her grew when she held my gaze, didn't retreat. That was a good indication her dislike for me had lessened. When she licked her lips, I knew she was mine.

"If you refuse me, Sarah, I will leave this ship with my honor intact. If you refuse me, I will die." I bent my knee and lifted her body off the floor so she rode my leg, her clit and pussy rubbing my thigh through our uniforms. "But death means nothing to me. I've been fighting the Hive for ten years, woman. I'm not afraid to die."

She shook her head slightly, as if trying to clear a lust-filled haze. "I don't understand why you are here. Can't you go find a woman on Atlan who actually wants a mate?" With her arms over her head and her hot core pressed to my thigh, she was spread before me like an offering, but I would not take her, not yet.

"*You* are my mate. I want *you*. I want you because you are the *one* for me. I feel it. The first time I saw you I wanted to throw you over my shoulder and carry you away."

"Because a woman can't fight," she bickered.

"Obviously a woman *can* fight. I just believe they *shouldn't*. It's not that. I wanted to carry you away because I wanted to press you up against the nearest wall and fuck you. Something like this." I nudged her core with my thigh. "And preferably without clothing or your team watching."

Her mouth fell open and her eyes dilated. The rise and

fall of her breasts sped up as she fought her body's craving, her need of me, fought the call between matched mates.

"Do not deny your desire for me as well."

She sputtered, looked at my chest, the floor. Anywhere but at me. "I don't even know you."

"Your body *knows* me. Your soul knows me as well. In time, your heart and mind will catch up. That's what's special about mates. Our connection, it's visceral. It's so deep, so permanent, that it defies logic. There is no room for doubt, for we *know* we are meant for each other."

She shook her head, her eyes closing as I tensed my thigh muscles, rubbing her core with my heat and strength.

"Do you deny the... connection?" I asked.

She shook her head, her hair rubbing against the wall. "You know I can't."

"Can't what?" I asked, running my lips along the delicate curve of her jaw, the swirl of her ear, the rapid pulse thrumming in her neck. I could smell her. Sweat, definitely, but something musky and feminine that soothed and aroused the beast inside.

"Can't deny you." My heart leapt at her words, words I had feared would never fall from her lips.

"Ah, Sarah. Such an admission was hard for you. I will keep it safe, guard it as I will you. Do not fear... our bond. While I need to fuck you to survive, there is time. I will honor your need for time, at least for now. I will not take you until you allow it, until you beg my cock to fill you."

She moaned and I pressed my advantage.

"But now, I want to kiss you, Sarah. I need to taste you."

She opened her eyes and the anger, the resistance was gone from her gaze. My beast wanted to howl at the submission I saw in her soft gaze. My Sarah, she fought so hard to be tough, to be a warrior. She was strong, yes. But she didn't have to be, not all the time. I was here for her now, to share her burden, to take on her troubles. Protect her from danger. She was also mine, mine to fuck, mine to tame, and mine to protect... she just didn't understand it yet.

CHAPTER SIX

Dax

I waited, our breaths mingling, her lush thighs squeezing mine.

Instead of replying, she tilted her chin and her mouth met mine.

In that moment, that instant, the beast came out. He took over the kiss, one hand tangling in her hair, cupping her head and tilting her just the right way to take the kiss deep and hard. My tongue filled her mouth, finding hers and tangling, tasting, licking. Her flavor only enhanced my need and I pressed my thigh into her more, hoping she'd use it, to ride my leg and find her pleasure. She didn't deny me this, for she squirmed and pushed off with her toes to move herself against me as I kissed her and kissed her.

Her lower lip was as plush and decadent as I'd suspected. Her body was soft, even beneath the body armor, and a perfect fit for mine. My beast raged for more, not wanting to stop at just this wild kiss. Even though my body craved more, this was not the time or place and I held the beast back. Lifting my head, I took in Sarah's closed eyes, flushed cheeks, swollen, red lips. A growl rumbled in my chest and her eyes opened, cloudy with desire.

"I want you. I want to bury my cock deep in your wet pussy and fuck you until you can't walk. I want to hear my name on your lips as you milk my seed." I tugged on her bottom lip with my teeth, slightly sharper because of the beast, then soothed the slight sting with my tongue. "I want to taste you, Sarah, everywhere, hold you down and lick your pussy until you scream your pleasure."

She laughed then and I wanted to kiss her all over again. "We don't even like each other."

"I think we like each other just fine." I swiped my thumb over her cheek, then stepped back. I didn't want to do so, but she was a dangerous challenge my beast didn't want to resist, even without her ion pistol aimed at me.

"We don't like the predicament we are in," I added. "You are the only female who can keep me from dying and I might just be the only one who can help you save your brother."

She bit her plump lower lip and frowned. "How? The commander has already forbidden us both from going after him."

"Actually, there is a solution," I replied, ignoring my desire to tug that lip from her straight teeth. I unbuckled the cuffs from my belt and held them up. "Mating cuffs. You see I'm already wearing mine. Wearing them shows I am committed to my mate—you—and only you. No one who sees them will doubt my claim." She looked at the gold bands dangling from my fist, but her hand lifted to wrap around the metal that encased my own wrists, her soft exploration making me shudder. I wanted her hand on me in other places.

"What's their purpose?"

"The cuffs are a form of commitment, an outward sign of mating. They ensure we remain in close proximity until the mating fever is gone and we are well and truly bonded. Atlan mating cuffs are recognized throughout the coalition. No one will doubt who you belong to, ever again. Just as all who see me will know I am yours."

"You can't take them off?"

I shook my head, willing her to understand. "They mark me as yours, mate, until the fever is over. Then, then they can be removed, but we will still be mated. That will *never* change. With these on, it indicates I am claimed. Mated. Taken. I have chosen a female. You." I rattled the smaller pair of cuffs dangling from my grip. "These are yours. Become my mate and together we can still save your brother."

Her mouth fell open and I could practically see her brain working.

She crossed her arms over her chest, not from defiance, but for personal protection. She was upset and unsure and was practically hugging herself. Had she ever had someone hold *her*? Protect her? Shield her from the evils of life? Was she so strong because she wanted to be, or because the men in her life had left her vulnerable and exposed?

"The commander won't allow us to go."

"That is true, so long as we both remain officers of the coalition fleet. It is also true, mate, that a rescue mission for one soldier isn't wise. But if you put on my cuffs, then it indicates you are a bride and I am a mated Atlan. We will both be released from all military service."

"Just by putting on the cuffs?"

"If you put them on, you are committing to soothing my fever. Ending it. Remember, it's *mating* fever and so you would be committing to being my mate."

"The cuffs would end our military contract?"

I nodded. "We will no longer belong to the fleet, Sarah, but to each other. The rules and orders of the coalition commanders would no longer be ours to follow."

She looked at the cuffs but refused to touch them. But she was listening, and that's all I needed right now.

"I vowed to help you retrieve your brother. On my honor, I will assist you whether you choose to take my cuffs or not. However, if you do not declare yourself my bride and choose to go with me, you will be breaking a direct order from Commander Karter. If we are successful, you may retrieve your brother, but could very well serve several years in a coalition prison cell."

"Why are you doing this?" Her gaze locked to mine, demanding the truth. "Why are you offering any of this to me? Why risk your life for my brother? You don't even know us."

"Nothing matters to me but you." I spoke the words with vehemence, shocked to discover I spoke the truth. My desire to continue fighting the Hive had died the moment I saw her. Nothing mattered to me but winning her over, making her mine. I never would have imagined such a change of feelings in such a quick span of time. It had only been a matter of hours since I had said I didn't want a mate. Now, now I never wanted to be free of her. I didn't lower the cuffs, but kept them right where she could see them.

"I'm... I'm not like women from your planet, am I? How can you want me?"

"No," I affirmed. "The women of Atlan are gentle, Sarah. They nurture and heal, they do not fight. They do not have your fire."

"Is that what you want? A doormat?"

I frowned. "I do not know what a doormat is."

"A woman who never argues, who does every little thing you tell her to. A meek female."

Atlan women *were* meek. Meek not because they were forced to be that way, but because they were raised as such. They were happy in their roles, confident in their mates to care for them. But Sarah? She was most definitely not Atlan and I doubted she'd ever be meek.

I grinned. "You? Meek? I've known you all of two hours and I know for fact you are anything but."

She pursed her lips then and I saw color stain her cheeks.

"I never said I wanted a meek Atlan woman."

She didn't say anything, but looked at me with obvious doubt.

"I don't lie, Sarah. If you don't trust me, you can trust in the matching protocol. *That* can't lie. If I truly wanted an Atlan woman, I would have been matched to one. I want *you*. I want your fire to burn me from the inside out."

The kiss hadn't been enough. It had only offered a hint of what it would be like between us. Hot, volatile, passionate. I wanted to feel this woman beneath me. I wanted to feel the anger, the frustration, the intensity she carried about turn into passion. To have that passion directed at me. There was no doubt she was a fiery one and she'd be an eager, aggressive bed partner. I'd use that fierceness to bring her pleasure. There would be no gentle claiming. It would be rough and wild and I'd have to fight her every moment for control, but the battle would make her submission so much sweeter to taste. She'd fight herself, try to resist what she needed. That was a certainty. Not because I'd subdue her, but because I would test her limits, revel in making her squirm and discover her deepest desires.

I pushed now, leaning forward and taking her mouth once more, making sure she knew just how much I wanted her. I released my hold and slid my hands behind her back, pulling her body forward and higher on my thigh until we were pressed close and her stomach rubbed against my rock-hard erection. Her hands landed on my biceps, but she kissed me back, didn't push me away.

A knock sounded on the door and I pulled away, reluctant to lose intimate contact with my mate. I held her to me, her much smaller frame safe in my arms. I tried to be gentle despite the beast raging at me to throw her down on the floor, shred her armor, and take what was mine. "Say yes, Sarah. Be mine."

"You vow that you will help me find my brother if I say yes?" She flicked a finger against one of the cuffs, and they swayed beneath my hand.

"I do not lie. I would *never* lie to my mate. As you do not know this, or me, I offer you my vow." I placed my right hand over my heart, the cuffs dangling between us. "I will help you whether you accept my claim or not."

She looked at me for any kind of deception. There was none, for I would assist her, no matter her choice. If she refused me, I would simply go after her brother alone and save her from a coalition prison cell. I would perish, soon after. The beast within was close enough to taste. Without a mate, I would be destined for execution, but I would not force her decision. If I died, I would seek eternal rest on my own terms, with my honor intact.

If she said yes, if she placed my cuffs on her wrists, I had no choice but to go with her to find her brother, for not only had I given her my word, but once she put the cuffs about her wrists, we could not be apart, not until we were truly bonded.

Worse, if I betrayed her trust, she would never allow me to fuck her, let alone bond with her. Without it, I'd die.

She then, held all the power. We were both in a dilemma. We both needed the other. Each of us had a price that we were willing to pay. I would subject my mate to danger to find her brother. She would become my mate. Permanently. Based on the kiss, it would not be a hardship.

"Very well. I accept."

I groaned then, low and deep. Hearing those words from her lips soothed the beast in a way not even the kiss had. It paced and nudged to escape, but hearing her agree to be my mate soothed it. Me. All of me.

I went to the door and opened it for the commander. I knew he hadn't gone far. Not only was I a rogue ex-warrior who'd transported into a battle and ripped the Hive to pieces, but I was also the Atlan who wished to mate one of his top officers.

He entered and looked between the two of us.

"You can't accept the warlord's plan," he said. He was a shrewd man, knowing exactly what I'd offered her and what it would cost him.

"I already have."

"Captain, I have to question the wisdom of your

decision," the commander replied. "Be logical. Use that analytical mind of yours, Sarah. Your brother is gone. Don't make this sacrifice when there is no hope of getting Seth back alive."

"Seth's still alive. I can feel it. I gave my word to my father. I can't lose him, too. He's all I have left. I'm sorry, Commander Karter, but I have to find him." The last line was like a mantra falling from her lips. She tugged the bracers from her forearms and dropped them at her feet. Grabbing the cuffs, she pushed her shirt up to expose her forearms. Opening one then the other, she slipped the cuffs about her wrists. They sealed automatically and cinched securely about her delicate skin.

Flicking a gaze up at me, she tilted her chin then turned to the commander. "Now what?"

The commander sighed. "Captain Mills, you have donned the mating cuffs of an Atlan male, therefore effective immediately, you will be transferred to the Interstellar Bride Program. Your command position is relieved. You are no longer a member of the coalition fleet. You will hand over your ion pistol."

With precision, she pulled the weapon from her hip and gave it to the Prillon. She did not seem to doubt her decision. In fact, the finality of it seemed to harden her resolve.

Commander Karter turned to me. "Well, I guess you got what you came for." He ran a hand through his hair with a loud sigh. "Check in with Silva on the civilian deck. She'll assign you temporary quarters."

Sarah placed her hands on her hips. "We won't be staying. We'll transport immediately."

The commander shook his head. "I'm afraid that's impossible."

"What? I promise you, once we transport to where the Hive took Seth, we'll be out of your way."

"There's no more transport until thirteen hundred tomorrow, at the earliest." When her mouth fell open in shock, he added, "Magnetic debris field is moving through. It's too dangerous. The entire sector is shut down. No transport, no flights."

"No!" There would be no transport, no battle, no movement for almost sixteen hours. Normally, everyone in the battle group celebrated these freak magnetic storms, allowing for rest and forced relaxation. Sarah's gaze flew to mine and I could read her easily. She was worried about her brother, about the extra time the Hive would have to torture and modify him. But she was also wondering exactly what I was going to demand of her over the next sixteen hours while we waited.

If I couldn't take her to her brother, I could provide a worthy distraction. Perhaps a good, hard night of fucking would clear both our heads.

CHAPTER SEVEN

Sarah

I grabbed my bracers off the floor, turned on my heel, and left the commander's war room and my new *mate* behind.

So, I was mated to an Atlan warlord who kissed like a god? Whatever. Once I was out of the commander's office, I tugged at the cuffs, trying to work them off. I might be Dax's mate, I might have all but humped his hard thigh, but I didn't need to wear these darn things. I had put them on as part of the show for Commander Karter, not that I was going to go back on my word. I wasn't. Once Dax helped me get my brother back, I would try to be a good little wife. Based on the way he kissed, a one-night stand would be pretty darn hot. Until then? I didn't need these... I tugged and tugged... visible signs that I was connected to the warlord. Owned by him. *Belonged* to him. My word was more than enough.

I tried to pry them open. Nothing. Shit. They were snug, but at least I could get my fingers beneath the gold bands. Regardless, there was no give. Where the hell was the clasp?

I nodded at two warriors who saluted me as they passed

me in the corridor. They were probably the last two salutes I'd get, for I wasn't in the coalition fleet any longer. I'd made it two months, not two years. At least I wasn't dead. Although it's possible that being mated to... *him* might be worse.

He was brash and bold and that wicked grin only indicated a cockiness that drove me crazy. Somehow he could just breathe and I'd be angry. And horny. What was it about him? What was it about his kiss that made me insane? And *horny*. God, he *was* sex on a stick. Somehow he'd gotten me to *want* him to touch me. He'd told me what he wanted to do to me, cavemen level, carnal things—and I was thankful he'd done it in private—as I'd all but melted at his feet.

Not only that, I'd kissed him like a woman eager for his advances. At first, I'd kissed him back because, what the hell? Why not sample what he was offering? When his lips met mine, however, it was more like, *more. Give me more.* His rock-hard thigh had nudged between my legs and lifted me up so that he pressed perfectly against me. My pussy ached to be filled and my swollen clit had rubbed and awakened. Between his tongue in my mouth and the way I'd humped his leg, I'd been on my way to orgasm central. Shameless. He'd even growled as I'd gotten wet, like he could smell me or something.

No man had ever made me feel like that before. He'd had me pinned against the wall and completely at his mercy. I never liked being at *anyone's* mercy, but with Dax, with his kiss and his touch and his whispered words and his... God, the hard feel of his cock against my lower belly where the body armor didn't cover... I wanted it all.

But my decision to be his mate wasn't made in a sex haze. I agreed to his bargain because I wanted to find Seth. He would help me do it, and I wouldn't have to rot in prison for the rest of my life. With Dax's size, his bravery, his brawn, I knew he was the best chance I had of getting my brother back.

I took a deep breath, then started down the hall toward the ship's elevator. Dax was still in the commander's room, and I had no idea why. He'd follow me eventually, because we had a deal. He'd said he'd die without me, which meant his species was seriously messed up. Hell, I'd lived twenty-seven years without a husband and I was doing just fine.

Sure, my vagina was practically dusty from disuse, but who needed a man, and all the drama, when a powerful vibrator was available? A vibrator never pissed me off. Of course, the vibrator didn't have big hands, a rock-hard, muscled physique, or a very powerful demeanor. Nor kissed like there was no tomorrow.

Okay, fine. Dax was better than a vibrator. So far. I had no doubt I'd wish for the old reliable and silent dildo the first time I refused to act like a weak, silent wallflower.

"Ah!" I cried out, my cuffs suddenly radiating a stabbing pain into my wrists. "Fuck!" I stopped moving and wrapped my hand around a cuff. The pain didn't lessen, but radiated up my arms. It was like being electrocuted but unable to take your hand off the live wire. I wouldn't be surprised if my hair started to sizzle. What the hell had the warlord done to me?

Honeymoon over, I spun on my heel and stormed back down the hallway. Just before I got within the sensor's range of the commander's door, the pain stopped, but sharp tingles lingered. I shook my hands out, getting the blood to circulate. Maybe it was a loose wire in the cuff, a faulty connection or something? I took a deep breath, the pain disappearing entirely. Once again, I turned back around and started down the hall. I made it as far as last time and the pain returned. This time, I knew what to expect and I hissed with rage, not pain.

The asshole. What the hell was he doing? Was it remote control? Was he watching me now and laughing at me?

I marched back to the door, this time not stopping when it opened for me. Standing right where I left them were the two men. The commander looked me over and the warlord had a smug smile on his face.

"You've returned," Dax growled.

I lifted my hands. "Yes, it seems the cuffs you gave me are defective."

"Oh?"

"As if you don't know," I grumbled.

The commander chuckled, slapped me on the back on his way out of the room. "It's a good thing this little lover's quarrel is no longer my responsibility," he said, pissing me off more than Dax.

I pursed my lips and stormed out of the room, but this time I ensured Dax was right behind me.

We were alone in the hall. Only the soft hum of the ship's systems could be heard when I turned on him, ready to fight.

Dax held up his hands and spoke before I could yell at him. "I have done nothing to your cuffs," he told me. "They are functioning properly."

"They feel like electroshock therapy! That's not functioning properly." I tugged at them again.

"Unbonded Atlan mates who wear the cuffs must remain within one hundred paces of each other, otherwise their cuffs produce a… pain that demands a return to closeness."

"Closeness?" I yelled, I knew I was losing it, but being put on a leash like a dog pissed me off.

"Do you always shout?" he responded.

"Do you always hurt your mate?"

His expression, his entire demeanor changed at my question and he crowded me until my back was once more against the wall. I couldn't help my damn self, I stared at his lips, wondering if he'd kiss me again. "Sarah Mills of Earth, you are my *only* mate. The last thing I wish to do is cause you harm in any way. It is my job to protect you, my privilege to bring you only pleasure."

I blushed at the lingering feel of his mouth on mine, the way his hard thigh made my clit tingle and swell, but shrugged it off.

"Yet these… things," I waved my arms in the air, "hurt."

"Do you not think it hurt me as well?"

I glanced down at his wrists, at the gold cuffs there. "Yours caused pain, too?"

He nodded, a dark curl falling over his forehead. "We are mated and what hurts you, hurts me. What pleases you, pleases me. You cannot be more than one hundred paces from me without pain, but the restriction is placed upon both of us. I cannot be apart from you either until the fever is gone."

That meant fucking. Lots and lots of wild monkey sex kind of fucking.

I looked him over. "You seem fine now."

"The fever comes on at random. Like during the battle, I assure you, you will know when it is upon me again."

"If these cuffs hurt so dang bad, then why didn't you come after me?"

"Because while you might have been the leader of your squadron, I am the leader of our mating, and our mission to retrieve your brother."

I shoved my way free of him and began to pace the hallway. "*This* is why I didn't want a mate. *This* was why I didn't want to agree to being mated. Men and their rules. You are all completely irrational."

"You have only been in space two months. I have led coalition troops for over a decade. I know the Hive better than you do. I know *more* about what's required to get your brother back. And, I'm Atlan and you're not."

I didn't turn to look at him. I was angry and crazy and definitely losing it. I couldn't go farther than one hundred paces from this guy without terrible pain. Why hadn't he mentioned that *before* I agreed to put the cuffs on?

"Once we find your brother, we will settle on Atlan. I will show you my world. There are many experiences you have yet to enjoy. I would prefer we both survive to experience them."

"So you want me to follow your lead since I'm… new to space life."

"That's part of it, but I am an Atlan male and I am in charge. If that is not enough to soothe your pride, to make your surrender acceptable, I am also your superior officer."

"Not anymore. I'm a civilian now, remember?" I pursed my lips. Surrender? God, I was in trouble here because I surrendered to *no one*.

"The male is in charge, Sarah. It is our custom and the Atlan way of life."

"Yes, you told me what Atlan women are like."

"Yes, but you *want* me to be in control. You want your mate to lead." He lifted his hand to my cheek and tilted my face so I looked up, way up, into his eyes. "You do not need to fight, Sarah. No more. I am here now. I will take care of you, as you truly desire."

My eyes widened in disbelief. "I don't *need* a man to take care of me and I definitely don't *want* one!" I countered.

"You do, or we would not be matched."

"Do I seem like a woman who wants to be led around all the time?"

He cocked his head to study me. "No, but you did like it when I kissed you. You had no control then."

I winced because I couldn't deny my reaction to that kiss, at least not honestly. He was right. I had liked it when he'd pinned me to the wall and took what he wanted. What woman didn't want to be pressed up against a wall and fucked? What woman didn't want a dominant male in the bedroom? Where was the fun leading a boy around by his balls all the time? There wasn't any. But that didn't mean I wanted him to be the boss of me. I had enough bosses in my life. Commander Karter was just the latest in a long string of commander officers and he was a pain in my ass.

I didn't want to be legally bonded to one of them!

As for the kissing, I had to admit I wanted him to do it again, and not stop until we were both naked and spent. Not because he wanted to take the lead—in everything—but because I was only human and I had girl bits that longed for a real cock.

"So what happens now?" I patted the metal wall beside me, unable to resist goading the beast. "We get it on right here so I can cure your mating fever?"

His eyes narrowed and his jaw clenched. "While the idea of fucking you against that wall is appealing, I won't take you unwillingly, or in a public place."

"Why not?" I was relieved at his words, but couldn't help myself as I backed up and lifted my hands over my head. I pressed my back against the wall and stared up at him with a blatant challenge in my eyes. The need to test his control rode me like a demon. I had to know just how far I could push him, what kind of man I was dealing with.

He stalked toward me until the smallest possible sliver of air separated us. His scent invaded my head and I wanted to drown in it, he smelled too good, like dark chocolate and cedar, two of my favorite things. I licked my lips as I held his gaze, daring him to do something crazy, daring him to break my trust.

His voice was a whisper. "Because you are mine, and no one will see your naked flesh but me. No one will hear your cries of pleasure when I take you. Your skin is mine. Your breath is mine. Your hot, wet pussy is mine. The whimpering pleas that I will force from your throat are mine. I will not share."

I couldn't breathe, was drowning in him and the erotic promise of his words.

"But know this, mate, if you continue to defy me, to tempt me to dishonor you, I will pull this armor from your soft body and bend you over my knee. Nor will you lie to me. I will have respect, Sarah Mills, or your bottom will be a bright, hot red before I fill you with my cock."

What the hell? I tried to process that as he tilted his head and studied me. My pulse was like a drumbeat in my ear as I fought to recover from his dark declarations, all of them, for suddenly the idea of his firm hand on my bottom made me squirm, and not out of anger. Damn him, he noticed.

"Does it arouse you to be spanked?"

"What? No!" I replied, his words like a bucket of cold water thrown over my head. "Don't you dare even think about it, Dax of Atlan."

He grinned then and he looked more handsome than ever, and my breath caught in my throat. "You want me, woman. You want my hard cock filling you. You want me to touch you everywhere, claim you, mark you as my own. Admit it."

"No. I don't want a mate, Dax. I want to save Seth." I shook my head but my heart was pounding so loudly I was sure he could hear it, even through my armor. I didn't want his words to be true, but they were. Holy hell, I did want it. I wanted all of it. But not until I had my brother back safe and sound.

"I will help you retrieve your brother. I gave you my word." He leaned in, not giving me any air. "You want me to take care of you, too, to keep you safe."

"No, I don't. I take care of myself."

"Not anymore."

"This is bullshit, Dax." I shoved against his chest. "We've got to go. We've to a rescue mission to plan."

"You are the most difficult female I've ever met."

I pushed my finger against his chest. "You are the most pigheaded, chauvinistic, arrogant—" The dark gray scrollwork that adorned the bright gold cuff taunted me as I poked at him. It was a sign of ownership, like a collar on a dog. Wrapping my hands about my wrist, I tugged at the stupid cuff. "Get these things off of me. I've changed my mind."

I heard a growl rumble from his chest. He took hold of my wrist and tugged me down the hall. He was searching for something. When he pressed an entry button, a random door slid open and he shoved me inside. The room's motion sensor turned on the light and I could see that he'd pushed me into a narrow room full of electrical panels. I had no idea what they did, but one wall was covered in cables and blinking lights. The floor and other walls were blue, indicating this room was maintained by engineering.

"What the hell, Dax?" I said, followed by a long string of swear words.

"Put your hands on the wall." He looked over his shoulder and pressed a button beside the closed door, engaging the lock.

My mouth fell open. While the suggestion was pretty hot—at least in connection with the pervy thoughts his command brought about—now I was pissed.

"I don't know what you think you're doing, but I'm not fucking you in a closet."

"Who said anything about fucking?" he responded calmly.

"Then what are you doing?"

"I'm going to spank you, of course."

I pressed my back against the wall opposite the electric panels, my hands flat on the cool metal. "What?" He was truly out of his mind.

"You need it." Dax took a step closer. Damn it, he was so big and this room was so fucking small.

"I need what? A spanking?" I laughed then. "Yeah, right."

"You lied to me, repeatedly. I warned you, mate. You are mine now, and I will do whatever I need to do to make sure you know that."

"You are crazy. Are all Atlan males this difficult, or is it just you?"

"You are still lying to me, and to yourself. In time, mate, you will come to me and tell me when you are scared, when you need my touch to soothe you, to ease your panic. Until then, it is my job to know when you need a firm hand."

"On my ass? I think not."

"You won't admit you're scared, that everything that has happened today is overwhelming. You are strong. I know this. But I am stronger. You can trust me to take care of you, Sarah. You are lashing out instead of admitting the truth. You dare me to discipline you with your lack of respect, your insults of my character and my honor. I can only assume you need me to take control but do not know how to ask me to do so. And so I will not wait for your admission, Sarah, I will simply give you what you need."

His promise made my stomach lurch. He was so big, huge even. He was an alien, an Atlan warlord in charge of hundreds of soldiers, thousands. And as much as I tried to put on a brave face, I *was* terrified. My brother was most likely dead, as the commander had said, or on his way to becoming one of the Hive. I couldn't fail him. Now I was mated to Dax and I wasn't a *normal*, meek Atlan woman. Surely I would fail him as well. As soon as he realized I wasn't what he wanted, he'd rip the cuffs off his wrists and send me packing. I'd go home alone and defeated. Lost. All my family gone.

I felt the first tear burn a trail down my cheek and shook my head in denial, turning away from Dax so he wouldn't witness my weakness, so he wouldn't know that he was right. I *did* need him to take control. The pressure was crushing me, suffocating me, and the idea of letting go, of surrendering... everything to someone else was like a seductive drug in my system. My mind screamed that it was wrong, but my heart pounded with both fear and longing, the war within threatened to tear me in two.

"Put your hands on the wall, Sarah."

I only shook my head. While I craved it, it didn't mean I'd let him know it. I must stay strong. I could hear my father's voice in my head, demanding I never cry, never show fear or pain. *You have to be tough, Sarah, the world won't tolerate weakness.*

Dax took a step closer, easily hooked a hand about my waist and spun me about. I had no choice but to place my hands on the wall, afraid I was going to fall. He tugged on my hips and pulled them out so I was bent at the waist. I started to rise, but a big hand came down on my pants-covered bottom.

"Dax!" I cried, stunned by the surprising burn of his palm against my ass.

"Leave your hands where they are. Ass out."

"I will not let you—"

Smack!

"You are not letting me do anything. I am giving you the spanking you need and you have no choice."

His hands came around to the front of my pants and worked them open, then tugged them down along with my panties over my hips, then left them around my thighs. I felt cool air on my bare ass and I knew it stuck out for him to see.

"Dax!" I cried again, feeling more vulnerable than ever.

He didn't leave me like that for long, but began to spank me then, swatting one side of my ass, then the other, never hitting the same place twice. It wasn't overly hard, for I could only imagine how hard he could truly strike if he wanted. That didn't mean it didn't hurt, that my skin wasn't heating up like fire.

"I am here for you. I'm not leaving you. I will find your brother. I will take care of you. I know what you need. You will not lie to me. You will not speak to me in a disrespectful tone. You will not deny your body's needs or our match again." He struck over and over as the tears streamed down my face in a river of anguish I felt like I'd bottled up for years, each swat of his hand like an emotional grenade as my control snapped.

I clenched my fingers on the wall, but had no purchase. "Dax!" I cried yet again, but now my voice was filled with raw emotion, not anger.

"No one is coming into this room. No one can see us. No one will think you are weak. Stop trying to deny what you need. Stop hiding from me. Let go."

I shook my head then. "No."

His hand stopped briefly, stroked over my heated flesh. "Ah, Sarah Mills, say these words: I don't always have to be strong."

After a minute, his hand patiently caressing my heated skin, I finally whispered, "I don't always have to be strong."

"Good girl." He spanked me again and I startled. "I will be honest with my mate and myself."

I repeated his words.

"I can trust that my mate will take care of me."

I said those too and the spanking, in my mind, changed to something else. He wasn't slapping my ass because he was punishing me, he was doing it because he had recognized something in me I'd never known existed. I had no idea how or why I needed a spanking, but just knowing that I was bent over and Dax was giving me no choice in it, that he was making me forget about everything, was liberating. The stinging swats had a wonderful ability to shut off my mind and I could trust that he was watching out for me. No harm would come to me as he did this. No one would see that my ass was bare and probably turning bright red. No one would see the tears on my cheeks. No one would see me, no one but Dax.

He wasn't laughing at me. He wasn't thinking I was weak. He was giving me a moment where nothing could hurt me and I could just forget it all. He was helping me release pent-up stress and emotions I wasn't even aware had been choking me. Regret. Fear. Rage. Guilt. It was all in there, swirling like a tempest in my chest, pouring out of me in the tears streaming down my cheeks until I was empty, but calm, like the sea after a storm.

"I belong to Dax and he belongs to me," Dax added.

I repeated the words, too tired to fight him or my own body's desire. But his next words changed the mood in the room from calm to hot in the blink of an eye.

"Dax is mine. His cock is mine."

I almost groaned at the dark tone of his words, my thoughts drifting to images of him fucking me from behind, right here, right now, in this stupid little closet. I repeated his words and the spanking stopped. I thought he was done, but his hand cupped my hot flesh, then slipped between my legs, over my folds to explore the heat I knew he'd find. He growled when his fingers encountered the wet welcome.

"My pussy belongs to Dax."

I gasped as he slid two fingers inside me, then repeated the words. He leaned over my back so that his massive form pressed into me.

"You're dripping wet, mate. I could fuck you now. Right now."

His fingers slipped in and out of my empty core and I arched my back. All his carnal words had me primed for him. That kiss, his hands on me, even the spanking, made me eager for him. I knew that he would take care of me, that in this moment, I had to think of nothing but his fingers deep inside of me.

"You were a good girl and took your spanking so well. Now you can come."

I groaned around a sob as he fucked me with his fingers, using two to stretch me open and one to rub my clit. As my tears dried, my mind blissfully empty for the first time in months, my body took over, needing release. Needing Dax to fuck me. I cried out as the first orgasm rolled over and through me, Dax's thrust so hard and deep my feet nearly left the floor. It was impossible to remain quiet as the walls of my pussy went into a full spasm around his fingers, greedy for more. My sweaty fingers slipped down the wall and Dax wrapped his free arm around my waist, lifting me up until I was suspended in midair, my back to his chest, his fingers deep inside me.

He wasn't finished with me and in seconds he'd pushed me to the brink again. I clenched down on his fingers as I came. Even after the ripples of aftershocks receded, he kept them still, but deep within. The pleasure, the stinging pain all coalesced and I cried again, tears I hadn't allowed to fall for years poured from my body like acid. I let it all out: grief over the death of my brothers and then my father, fear that I'd lose Seth, the stress of command, guilt over the men I'd lost in combat. It felt as if a lifetime of bottled pain exploded from me.

He slipped his fingers from me and pulled me into his arms, hugging me close. I couldn't remember the last time I'd been hugged, the last time I'd truly been held. Sure, I'd had sex before, but it had been fairly emotionless, more hot release than true, intimate connection. My father had kept me at arm's length, for he had not been a coddler. With three older brothers and no mother around, there had been no emotion, no tenderness in our house. It was more a *Lord of the Flies* existence, where only the strong survived. I'd never regretted my life, or my decisions. But being here, in Dax's arms, made me tired, mentally and emotionally exhausted in a way I'd never allowed myself to feel, in a way it had never been safe to feel.

How had one big brute of a space alien seen past my armor—and it wasn't the warrior clothing I was referring to—and known what I needed more. I was strong, perhaps too strong, and it had taken him all of ten minutes to crack me open like an egg.

Even against the hard plate of his chest armor, I could hear his heart beating. I was, for once, calm and remarkably at peace. *Nothing* was going to happen to me right now. I was safe and my mind was quiet.

"Better?" he asked, once my crying jag subsided.

"Better," I replied. My body was soft and pliant, my ass fiery hot and sore. But I felt like someone was paying attention to me, *for* me. I didn't know how, but I'd needed that spanking. Analyzing my reactions would just make me crazy, so I resigned myself to figuring that all out later.

I stiffened in his hold and realized my ass was sticking out. I tugged up my pants and fixed the fastening, once again putting myself to rights. I tried to walk away, shame chasing the contented glow from my mind the moment I'd lost his touch, but he stopped me with a hand on my chin, lifting my face to look at him.

"Watching you come is the most beautiful thing I've ever

seen." His thumb stroked my cheek and I couldn't help it, I leaned into his touch as he continued. "You are mine. You will never be alone, never sleep alone, never fight alone. You are mine and I will never leave you."

"Dax. I can't think about that right now. I just can't. I have to save Seth."

"We will save Seth."

"Okay. We will save Seth." As much as I hated to admit it, having him help me was a huge relief.

"And then you will come home with me and we will begin a new life."

I nodded, unable to deny him right now. All my carefully constructed walls were gone, torn down by my new mate with his strength and iron will.

"Good, because I want your throaty little sighs of pleasure just for my ears. Your pussy walls all but milked my fingers, but I want to feel you come on my tongue. I want to taste your mouth and your pussy. I want to hold you down and fill you with my cock until you beg me for release, and I want to make you come over and over until you beg me to stop."

Holy shit, that was hot. Dax was blatant and completely unashamed in his desire for me. I'd never felt anything more real, more intense.

I felt his cock, hard and thick, against my belly. "What... um, what about you?"

He held up my hand and traced a path of dried blood that colored my skin, a reminder of all that we'd done today. "The mating fever could come upon me at any time. When it comes, my actions may be beyond my will to control. Just know that you are the only one who can soothe it. I will fight not to take you if you are resistant, but my life will be in your hands. *You* may have to take *me*."

I imagined him flat on his back as I rode him like a wild woman, his cock thick and deep as I ground my hips against his, taking what I wanted from him. I couldn't shake the idea of having this strong, powerful warlord on his back and between my thighs, mine to take. When he added a sly grin at the end of his declaration, I knew that while he was serious, he was also flirting. This big space alien covered in Hive blood was actually flirting with me. For once, I had no comeback.

· · · · · · ·

Sarah

A sound woke me. I stared into the darkness trying to figure out what it was, where I was. I had on the usual tank top and shorts, my normal sleeping gear. The bed was soft and the constant hum of the ship's systems didn't allow me to forget I was no longer on Earth.

There, I heard it again. Someone was in the room.

"Lights, half power."

The room brightened.

It all came back to me in a quick rush. I was in temporary housing quarters with my new mate, waiting for the magnetic storm to clear so we could transport. The room only had the one bed, no couch or other chair, forcing us to share. I was unaccustomed to sleeping with a man—usually a one-night stand didn't include a sleepover. But this wasn't a quick roll in the hay, this was my mate, and I'd fallen asleep with his huge body wrapped protectively around mine. While the bed was large, so was Dax, and I'd given up protesting when he pulled me against him and drifted to sleep.

Now, though, the sheets were a wild tangle. I was in bed but Dax was sitting on the floor in the corner. His hands were clenched into fists, his neck was arched, his bare chest glistened with sweat and his fingers tapped out a frantic pace against the floor.

"Don't move. I won't be able to save you," he growled.

Worry cut through me but I stilled. "What's wrong? A nightmare?" I knew many fighters who struggled with nightmares from the horrors of battle.

"The fever. Don't come closer unless you want me balls deep and out of control."

I remembered the strength he'd displayed as he grabbed the Hive soldier and ripped his head off. I worried my lower lip between my teeth as I wondered just how dangerous he was. "Do you think you'll hurt me?"

"I don't know what the beast will do, Sarah. I've never had the mating fever before. It can sense you, smell you. It wants you and you're there," he pointed at me, "in a bed and wearing just that skimpy clothing, your nipples hard. I can smell you—"

He shut his eyes to block me out.

He wouldn't hurt me. Deep down, I knew that. I have no idea where the knowing came from, but instinct told me he wouldn't hurt me. Not now, not ever.

Dax's sleep pants were black and the loose material did nothing to hide the rigid outline of his cock. It tented his pants and it proved *all* of him was large. He'd said that the fever brought about rage, anger, the need for sex.

"You said it was the mate's job to soothe the beast," I replied, sliding from the bed and crawling toward him. "And you said I could ride you, Dax. You promised me."

Every line of his body was tense, taut with restless energy and need. He was like a male model, all defined, hard muscles. His broad shoulders tapered into a narrow waist, a smattering of dark hair was between his brown nipples and tapered to a thin line that went beneath the band of his pants. He didn't have six-pack abs, but eight. He didn't need body armor to be rock hard. And lower, God, lower, his cock was like a hammer beneath the fabric of his pants. I physically ached to touch him, to feel the softness of his skin, the heat of it, the springy feel of his chest hair. The thickness of his cock. The *taste* of it.

"I don't think you can soothe this, Sarah. When full mating fever is upon me—and this isn't even it—the only way I can be soothed is to fuck. Not once, not twice. Again and again until I've finally burned off the restless energy, the need."

I had no idea why the idea of having Dax unleashed was so appealing. I should be fearful, just as he cautioned, but I wasn't. Not after the way he'd seen to me earlier. He'd spanked me, then made me come. While he'd been dominant, he hadn't been hurtful. It had been... exhilarating when I'd finally relinquished control to him, when I finally understood that I didn't have to be strong for him.

So while he was trying to be strong for me, it was my turn to give him what he needed. *I* was the only one who could.

"So you want to take me hard?" I asked. The very idea of him taking me without finesse had my pussy weeping.

His eyes were on my body. My tank top was snug, clearly outlining my bare breasts as I crawled toward him, my nipples already hard.

"Yes." His eyes narrowed and the pupils were all but gone, leaving complete black.

"You want it rough?" I crawled closer. Perhaps we *were* perfectly matched, for I couldn't imagine anything hotter than Dax going wild, which meant I wanted it that way.

"Yes." His palms slid over the floor as if trying to grab something, anything, but me.

"You need me to take the edge off?" I had a few needs of my own. I *needed* to come once or twice.

"*Yes.*"

I felt powerful and desirable and my pussy dripped with a returned need. The way he'd fucked me with his fingers, made me come from them alone, had me wanting more. Now, now I wanted it as much as he did. I should walk away. I should *run* away, for I truly didn't know this man. I was going to have sex with a stranger, an oversized alien with mating fever who wanted to fuck and fuck and *fuck*.

Hell, every Earth woman would kill to be me. I couldn't skip this opportunity. My inner walls clenched with the demand to be filled with his huge cock. I glanced down at it and I saw the way pre-cum had seeped from the tip to wet the clinging fabric. I could clearly see the outline of the broad crown and the start of the thick vein that ran down the length.

"You must take me, Sarah. If I have you beneath me, I might hurt you."

My eyes narrowed with desire. I was on my hands and knees before him. "You want me to ride you?"

He didn't answer with words, but tugged at the drawstring at his waist and pushed his pants down over his cock. It sprang free and I couldn't help but swear at the sight of it.

"Holy shit."

It was the biggest cock I'd ever seen. Porn star worthy. He'd certainly hidden it well in his uniform pants. It was thick and very hard, the skin taut and a dark rose color, filled with blood. Clear fluid gathered at the narrow slit at the top. Dax gripped the base in his hand and began to stroke it.

"Just having you look at my cock makes me want to come."

I watched as he pumped his fist and I swear his cock got even bigger.

"I'm not sure… I'm not sure that's going to fit."

He offered me a pained smile. "Take off your shirt, Sarah."

I arched a brow, then grinned. "For wanting me to fuck you, you're awfully bossy."

"I'm going to rip it off you in about three seconds. I just figured you'd want something to wear when I'm finished with you."

He had a good point and the way his free hand was gripped into a fist, I didn't doubt he'd snag the neckline of the shirt and rend the fabric.

Sitting back on my heels, I lifted it over my head, letting my hair slide free and down my back.

I shifted so I could get my shorts off. When I dropped

them on top of my shirt, Dax groaned.

I knelt before him in just my panties. I didn't know if Atlan women had panties or not, but since I was from Earth, they were allowed as part of my uniform. They were plain white, not the least bit enticing or sexy, but the way Dax was looking at me, it was as if they were the most delicate of lace and satin.

My nipples tightened under his gaze.

"Touch yourself. Show me what you like," he growled, his eyes glued to my breasts.

I placed a hand on my belly and his eyes lowered to it. I moved it upwards and over one breast, then the other. While it felt good to watch as his gaze followed my hand, I wanted *his* touch.

He slowly shook his head. "Not there. Lower."

My clit pulsed, agreeing with him.

I slid my hand back down and then beneath my panties, my fingers brushing over my clit. It was swollen, so swollen that just brushing it made my mouth fall open, my eyes closed.

"Eyes on me, Sarah." His voice was a dark growl.

I looked at him, saw the feral need there, the heat, the longing.

"Are you wet?"

I bit my lip and nodded, the slick essence coating not only my lower lips, but now my fingertips.

"Show me. Prove to me that you're ready for my cock. That you want it."

I lifted my hand up and he could see my wetness coating my fingers. He groaned then, his restraint had weakened and he grasped my wrist and tugged me forward. I placed a hand on his shoulder for balance and widened my knees.

He took my fingers into his mouth and sucked my sticky juices off. This was the most erotic thing... ever.

"Dax," I moaned his name as the suction of his fingers made me wonder what that mouth would be like on my pussy.

"You taste sweet," he growled. "Now, Sarah. It needs to be now. Knowing you want it, too, makes it harder for me to control myself. If the beast escapes, he won't stop."

He released his hold and I placed that hand on his other shoulder. While he was obviously raging with fever, he'd waited until he knew I was ready for him, that my pussy was so wet that it could take his big cock. Even now with his fever riding him, he'd ensured I would not be hurt.

When he straightened out his legs, I was suddenly straddling him. Raising his hands to my hips, he curled his fingers into the sides of my panties and tugged, ripping them from me. I was completely exposed, completely naked.

Moving my knees forward, I positioned myself so I was directly above his cock. Slowly, carefully, I lowered myself down until the blunt head bumped into my pussy.

He hissed and I moaned. His hands came to my hips and gripped tightly. I would surely have bruises there come morning.

"Now, Sarah. Holy fuck. Now."

Reaching down between my legs, I parted my slick folds around him and lowered my body over his thick head. He was so big that I bit my lip at the sharp sting of pain as he stretched me open, filling me. It had been a long time since I'd been with anyone, and he was not the average man.

I clenched his shoulders. He was staring down between my legs and I lowered my head to see what he was looking at. A little at a time his cock was disappearing inside me. It was such an erotic sight as I took more and more.

Taking deep breaths, I tried to relax and let gravity help. Bending his knees, he made a cradle for me to sit within, gave me a place to lean. As I used his thighs for leverage, the angle of my body shifted slightly and he slid deep in one smooth glide, not giving me time to adjust. All of a sudden I was simply full. Too full.

I cried out, my forehead on his chest as I tried to breathe, squirming on him, trying to pull off. "It's too much. You're too big."

He soothed me with his hands on my back, keeping me still. "Take a minute to adjust. You're perfect for me. You'll see. Just being inside you is helping. I won't hurt you. I promise. I am big and your pussy is so tight. It's so wet and eager for me. Clench down on me. Yes, just like that."

As he continued to talk to me, I relaxed, adjusted to the huge feel of him. I'd *never* had such a big cock before. I had no doubt that as soon as I began to move, I'd be completely ruined for all others.

All of a sudden I wanted to lift up, to move on him. Remaining still was instant torture. Moving, I pulled back, then dropped down, making Dax groan.

"Again."

I did it again. And again.

"Don't stop."

He didn't have to tell me that, for I had no intention of stopping. I began to ride him in earnest, lifting up and slamming down hard; every time I moved, my clit rubbed against him. I tilted my head back with abandon, knowing that he wasn't going to let me go, he wasn't going to do anything but let me fuck him until I came, until I made *him* come.

My breasts bounced and swayed as I moved, but I didn't care. I knew he could feel the soft flesh at my hips beneath his fingers, but I didn't care. I didn't care about anything.

I'd never been so hot, so eager for someone before. Usually I needed tons of foreplay before I could even consider fucking. For Dax, I just had to hear his voice, see his cock and I was dripping wet.

"I'm going to come," I cried, moving my hips in small circles, grinding on him.

"Good girl. Come for me. Come for your mate."

I screamed as I came, the pleasure of it making my fingertips tingle, my toes numb. My thigh muscles quivered and sweat broke out on my skin. There wasn't a more vulnerable moment and I could feel Dax's hands holding me tightly, the warmth and solidity of him beneath me.

When I caught my breath and opened my eyes, Dax remained buried deep, still hard and thick. He grinned at me. "You're beautiful when you come."

I flushed at his compliment.

"The fever is soothed a bit," he breathed. I couldn't tell by looking at him. His hands still tightly gripped my hips, the cords in his neck were rigid and his cock had certainly not diminished.

I frowned. "But... but you haven't come."

"Just being inside you seems to help. Seeing you come *definitely* helped. I have never had the fever before, so I am learning, too. Do not fear, I am in control again."

"I don't want to stop." I could still ride him, still fuck him to orgasm. I could come again. I wanted to come again, like a naughty, naughty girl. I wanted more. "I... I don't want you in control."

"You have done your job well as mate, soothing my inner beast." His hands lifted to cup my breasts, his thumbs brushing over my nipples and I leaned into his touch as fire shot straight from my breasts to my clit. "Now, *I* am going to fuck *you*. But first, I want to taste you. "

Before I could respond, he lifted me up so his cock came free. He moved so that he lay flat on his back on the hard floor. Instead of straddling his waist, I straddled his... his face.

I looked down at him between my thighs, saw the gleam in his eye, the wicked grin on his lips.

"Dax," I said breathlessly.

"I can still taste you on my tongue from when I licked your fingers. Your pussy juices ease the fever. It's like medicine. I need more."

He stopped talking then, took hold of my hips and lowered me so I was sitting on his face.

I had nothing to hold onto and I fell forward as my hands slapped against the wall. I looked down at Dax's dark head and watched as his tongue flicked over my clit before he took it into his mouth and sucked. I was right. His tongue *was* much better than my fingers.

"You're going to come for me and then I'll fuck you."

His voice was muffled by my thighs. He kissed one, then nipped it, making me gasp. He was being bossy and I didn't mind it at all. Apparently, being commanded to come by a man with his mouth on my pussy made the authority issue I had much easier to overlook.

"Okay," I replied, for what woman would refuse another orgasm?

I gave over then, for my only alternative was to climb off him, and that was *not* going to happen. He was a talented lover, wielding his tongue like a master artist. My clit was already sensitive and the gentle flick of his tongue, the full suction of his mouth pushed me to the brink, and over, quickly. He left me wilted and panting, sweating and sated.

"Cock. I need your cock," I admitted.

As if I were a doll, he easily lifted me up and carried me to the bed. He placed me on my stomach and tucked my knees beneath me. My cheek was on the cool sheets and my bottom was up in the air.

I felt the soft press of his cock against my pussy. He slid it up and down over the slick, swollen flesh.

"This is what you want?"

I gripped the sheets and looked over my shoulder at him. The pants were gone and I could see his legs. Pure muscle curved over his tall frame. Lean hips tapered to a narrow waist, then a solid, broad chest. He was like Michelangelo's David, if he'd carved a space man.

I pushed back against his cock, wanting it inside me and not willing to wait. "Yes."

The broad head nudged against all my tender flesh, even pressed against my back entrance, where I'd had nothing go before. "Here, Sarah. When I am fully in control, I will want you here. The beast will command your pussy. He will think only of breeding you, of tying you to him forever." He stroked my back entrance with his thumb, taunting me with his erotic thoughts. "But I will want to explore all of you, mate. Every inch of your body will be mine to taste, to claim, to fuck." He slid inside my wet heat in one hard, fast thrust and I clenched down, thinking about how big he felt in my pussy. I couldn't imagine him taking me in such a private place.

"I've never... I haven't—" I admitted.

"I want all of you." He leaned over my back until his mouth rested just behind my ear, his body covering me as his cock pumped in and out of my body. "You are mine."

"Yes."

He moved off me and walked to the wall. I rested my cheek on the cool sheets and tried to ignore the empty feeling in my pussy, tried not to think about how badly I wanted him back where he belonged, inside me, making me come.

Still, this view had its advantages. I admired what was mine, watched the muscles in his perfect ass flex and tighten as he walked away.

"What are you doing?" I asked. Didn't he want to finish? Was he done with me?

"I forgot you are not from my world and have not been prepared for an Atlan lover."

I frowned.

"Atlan females are prepared from their eighteenth birthday in the ways of pleasing a mate. To be ready for his mating fever. She is prepared in the art of fucking. All fucking."

"You mean—"

He pressed a few buttons on a wall unit and returned with a small box. Returning to me, he placed the box on the bed beside me, opened the lid.

My eyes widened when he showed me the butt plug. I'd never had anything shoved up there before, but that didn't mean I didn't know what one was.

"All fucking, Sarah. Pussy, mouth, and ass. Have you sucked a cock before?"

He pulled out a tube of something that looked like

lubricant.

"Yes," I replied, but not a cock as big as his. I definitely couldn't take it all. Not even a porn star could handle all that.

"And your ass? Do you have a virgin ass, Sarah?"

He squeezed a large dollop of the clear lube onto the plug. It was smaller than his cock, but I had doubts about its ability to fit in my bottom. I pushed up on my elbows.

"Back down, please. It's time to prepare this gorgeous tight hole. I'm soothed, temporarily, but I never want to hurt you. Only bring you pleasure." With one hand, he pulled one ass cheek away from the other, spreading my bottom wide open. "The way you respond to me, I have no doubt you're going to love taking my cock deep in your ass."

I blushed, knowing he could see all of me. "Says the man *not* getting a plug shoved up his ass," I grumbled.

I could hear his laugh, but he didn't relent. I felt the slippery, hard tip of the plug at my back entrance.

"No, says the man who's going to train his mate's ass for his cock, and if she's a good girl, fuck her long and hard. How many times can you come in a night, Sarah?"

I winced as he began to push the plug into me. It didn't hurt really, but felt very, very weird.

"Oh, um. Usually once, maybe twice if I touch myself."

He continued to work the plug into me, opening me wider and wider.

"Dax!" I cried, but it slipped into place then, my bottom clenching down on the narrow section. I could feel the wide handle pressing against my bottom.

"So beautiful." He swiped a finger over my folds. "So wet. You like it. I am so pleased that you gave in, that your body accepts what I give you."

"If you're in charge, then fuck me already."

He tapped the base of the plug and it came to life. Holy shit, it was a vibrating plug. Nerve endings I didn't even know I had came to life and I arched on the bed.

"See? The perks of an Atlan female. There are many of

them and I look forward to showing you every single one."

Yeah, this was one perk I definitely liked.

I started to squirm on the bed, the once soft feel of the sheets abrading my tender nipples. My clit swelled and I rubbed it on the mattress. I couldn't control the intense pleasure coming from my bottom. Holy shit, I was going to come just like this. "Dax!"

"You fucked me, Sarah. Now, it's my turn to fuck you. You'll take it. You'll take all of me because you're going to love it. Say the words."

I loved the way he was so overwhelming and dominant, and yet, he wouldn't take me without my agreement. He could shove a plug up my ass, but he wouldn't fuck me until I agreed. He would have stepped away from me if I'd said no. Even in his need to rut—as he'd called it—to soothe the fever, he was ensuring I was in the right mindset.

"I want it. God, please, I need it," I moaned, breathy and desperate. "You can't leave me like this!"

Carefully, he slid in, slowly, but in one long stroke. He bottomed out and I tossed my head back at the incredibly tight feel of his cock and the plug filling me up. I'd been full before when I rode him, but this angle, this position was so much deeper. The plug was tight, the vibrations making everything so fucking intense. It was *so* good.

He began to move then, sliding in and out at his pace, the way he wanted. "You see, Sarah, when I take charge, you like it. I control your pussy. I control your ass. You're going to come for me, again and again. Twice is not going to be enough. I'm going to wring every bit of pleasure from your body and you're going to give it to me."

I clenched down on him at the thought and gritted my teeth.

His hand came down on my bottom, hard. The loud smack filled the room.

I came then on a scream. The mix of the vibrations, his cock buried deep and the sharp, hot slap on my bottom pushed me over the edge. I clamped down on his cock, squeezing it, eager to pull it deeper into my body.

Leaning over me, his chest molded to my back as he placed a hand beside my head. "I can do anything I want and you *will* submit. Why?"

His hips continued to piston in and out of me as he continued his verbal porno. I was about to come again from just his words.

"Because you want me to take you. You need me to be in control. You need to submit as much as I need to dominate. You have no idea what I'm going to do next, but you still want it. We're perfect for each other."

"Yes!" I cried when he reached his hand around and settled my clit between two of his fingers and pinched.

His hips lost their measured pace and he began fucking me in earnest. Hard, rough. Short strokes. Hard breathing. I came again, pulsing around his cock. Once, twice, he filled me, then he nipped my shoulder as he came, stifling his groan and filling me with his hot seed. The little bite of pain only pushed me over into another powerful orgasm. I collapsed onto the bed as Dax pulled out and dropped beside me. The bed bounced and I rolled into him. I felt a slight press against the plug and the vibrations shut off.

I moaned at the lingering feeling of being completely dominated, well fucked, sated. We were sweaty and sticky, his seed slipping from me. My hair was a wild tangle and I was worn out, my body sensitive.

"Did that end your fever?" I asked sleepily sometime later.

"Mmm," he said. "No. But I am back in control. For now. The beast will return until he gets his turn fucking you."

"What does that mean, Dax?"

He sighed, and rolled onto his side so he could pet me, his huge hand running from thigh to shoulder and back again, lingering on all the soft, sensitive places in between. "Have you seen an Atlan in beast rage?"

"No." I relaxed under his touch, content beyond words

as his warm hand soothed me. "I thought maybe I saw something when you were on the freighter, but I wasn't sure."

"Yes." He pinched my nipple and I opened my eyes to find him watching me. "What did you see?"

It was difficult to talk with him rolling my pebbled nipple between his fingers, tugging and playing with me, but I tried, too well sated to resist. "You seemed bigger, like you grew. Your face looked meaner, too, more like a Prillon warrior, sharper somehow."

His hand moved from my nipple to explore the still wet folds of my pussy. When I held my legs together, he leaned over and nipped at my shoulder. "Open for me. Now. I want to feel my seed in your pussy. I want to touch you."

Good grief, the growl was back. Talk about a Neanderthal. He wanted to smear his seed all over me? Feel his claim deep, where he'd come inside me just moments ago? Fine. It wasn't like he hadn't seen, touched, tasted, and fucked every inch of me. And, the plug was still filling my bottom.

I spread my legs wide and his fingers pressed deep, the wet heat of our combined fluids brought a deeper growl from him as he filled me with two fingers and smeared his seed all over my pussy lips and thighs.

"When an Atlan goes into beast mode, his muscles can increase up to half again their size. His teeth appear to elongate as his gums retract and his mind becomes clouded in battle haze. Besides during mating, the haze usually comes when he is threatened, in battle, or when he is defending his mate."

He lazily rubbed my clit with his thumb and my hips jerked involuntarily. "You went beast because I was there?"

"Yes."

I stared at the ceiling trying to make sense of my new life as he played with my body, slowly bringing me back to life, making me ache for his cock yet again. God, his beast was going to fuck me? That huge, hulking brute who'd ripped the heads off Hive soldiers without breaking a sweat? What did that even mean, to be fucked by a beast? Was Dax truly going to be out of control? His mind gone? How big was he going to get? And why did the idea make me want to cross my legs and squeeze them to battle the rising heat in my body? My naughty little pussy wanted the beast's cock, wanted my new lover to be a little out of control.

"It appears my mating instincts have definitely kicked in."

Too embarrassed by the turn of my thoughts, I didn't open my eyes when I asked, "What instinct is that?"

"I feel like a victor, like I've won a battle as I watch my seed sliding from your swollen and well fucked pussy. To see the plug preparing your ass for me. Your eyes are glassy and your body limp, and I wish to beat my chest and roar knowing that I've pleasured you completely, that my cock filled you so full you will still feel my possession in the morning."

"Wonder of wonders, the male ego is the same everywhere," I countered, too well pleasured to take offense. "On Earth that's called being a caveman."

He growled and my eyes flew open as he pinned me beneath him, his hard cock sliding into my still dripping pussy in one slow, easy stroke. He pinned my arms above my head on the bed and fucked me slowly, the slow burn turning to instant fire as I wrapped my legs around his hips and whimpered. His gaze was intense and focused, watching every flicker of my eyelids, every breath as he rode me, claimed me, fucked me. Gaze locked to mine, he thrust hard and said, "And do you have a caveman on Earth, my Sarah?"

I considered teasing him, but immediately thought better of it as he pulled out and slammed hard and deep, actually moving me on the bed with the force of his thrust.

"No. You're the only caveman I've got."

He growled, his words barely recognizable. "You are mine."

Thrust.

"Mine."

Thrust.

He fucked me until I was desperate to come, until the word *please* actually fell from my lips.

He held perfectly still, his cock deep inside me and waited for me to meet his gaze. "Say my name, Sarah."

"Dax."

My reward was a strong thrust of his hips and I gasped. He stilled, reached between us and brought the vibrator in my ass back to life.

"My name?"

Oh, God. We were going to play this game?

I tried to lift my hips; he simply pinned me to the bed with his greater weight. My arms were locked above my head, my breasts thrust up and on display for his pleasure. I was out of options.

"My name?"

"Dax."

He moved then. My reward. His huge cock stretching me and stroking deep along the walls of my pussy, hitting that one special place that made me lose my mind. He didn't have to ask again.

"Dax. Dax. Dax."

"Good girl." He smiled and gave me what I wanted. Before he was done with me, his name filled the room like a chant.

CHAPTER EIGHT

Dax

"The coordinates for Captain Mills' location are programmed in." One of the transport attendants swiped a tablet, then looked at me. Looked *up* at me, for he wasn't very tall.

It took a moment to realize he wasn't referring to Sarah, but to her brother, Seth. Sarah was no longer a member of the coalition fleet, she was mine. I just needed to get her brother and get them both out alive.

Commander Karter had turned out to be halfway decent, allowing us to wear our armored uniforms. He'd even supplied us with ion pistols.

"You can't change your mind and come back to fight if you're dead," he'd said to Sarah. That was probably as sentimental as he was going to get, but I was thankful she was well protected for whatever we were going to face. I had the beast within me to help. If a Hive fighter was anywhere near Sarah, I would surely go into berserker mode and kill him with my bare hands. I had a weapon too, just in case, but I doubted I'd use it.

Even back in the body armor, there was no hiding her

curves, at least not from me. Perhaps I noticed them more because I knew exactly what her breasts looked like, how they felt in my hands, how her nipples tasted. Her hips appeared rounder, but that was because I knew how soft they were beneath my hands as she came all over my cock. It wasn't even the mating fever that was making me eye Sarah with barely suppressed desire. I was simply a man admiring a lush, desirable woman.

"Warlord, Officer Mills' last known location was aboard a Hive transport ship. There were beacons from several other coalition fighters pinging from there, which leads us to believe it is a prison vessel, or transport heading to an integration center."

"I've heard of the IC," I replied, not wanting to speak aloud of what the Hive did to prisoners there: made them part of their collective, implanted their biological bodies with synthetic technology that would take over both their bodies and their will. Made them slaves. Sarah's jaw clenched and I saw her blink back worry for her brother. That small display of her fear caused all desire to disappear.

"What direction is the ship traveling?" Sarah asked.

The transport officer flicked his gaze at Sarah, lingered on her breasts, then to me. "They are heading out of the system, toward Sector 438, warlord."

I saw Sarah's gaze narrow at the blatant snub.

I pointed to my mate. "She asked you the question."

"Yes, but *she* is no longer in the coalition fleet."

Sarah only shifted onto the balls of her feet, otherwise she displayed no outward sign of irritation. I, however, felt anger quite similar to the mating fever build inside me. This… attendant was patronizing and disrespectful to Sarah, to my mate.

"Neither am I," I countered.

"If the ship is heading toward 438, then it's heading for Hive-controlled space. Once it crosses over, they're lost. We won't have long to save them." Sarah ignored the chauvinist behind the transport control and spoke only to me.

The attendant's mouth fell open, then closed with an audible click at Sarah's information.

"Transport Attendant... Rogan." She glanced at his name tag on his uniform shirt. "When you make the transport, please change the coordinates from Captain Mills' exact location to two decks below."

The attendant frowned. "Two decks below?"

"Most likely they are holding my brother and any other prisoners in the brig, and we do not want to transport into a holding cell. We also do not wish to transport directly in front of the Hive. The brig is housed on level five of an IC transport. Two floors below is the supply floor, which you would know if you'd ever been on a recon mission aboard a Hive vessel. The fifth level is automated and usually not manned by Hive personnel."

She arched a dark brow, daring the man to doubt her.

"Is she correct?" I asked, my tone the one I used when I commanded an Atlan brigade.

He stiffened and glanced at me. "Correct. The Hive use robots to maintain and service their supplies," he replied.

"Then do as *former* Captain Mills ordered."

Her plan was a sound one. I was prepared to fight the Hive directly after transport, just as I had when I'd been sent directly to Sarah's coordinates. Neither the transport officer, Commander Deek, nor I considered exactly what I would be transporting into when they'd sent me to my mate. Neither of us assumed she would be in a battle at that very moment. It was a tactical error, for I'd put Sarah's team in danger and had caused Seth Mills to be captured by the Hive.

Had I considered what Sarah did now, the exact location not of our quarry, but of a safe place to transport, we most likely wouldn't be going on this dangerous rescue mission.

It was just her and me, but still, she was thinking like a true warrior and I felt something I had not expected to feel in regards to my mate's fighting skills... pride.

"Yes, warlord."

The transport attendant swiped his finger once, then twice and I looked at Sarah. "Ready?"

She nodded, then took my hand. I didn't have time to consider the gesture for in the blink of an eye we were no longer on the battleship, but in a barely lit room filled with hard-sided boxes. The deep hum of the machinery was constant, much louder and deeper than the usual cadence of a ship's systems. Immediately, Sarah dropped into a crouch. For a brief moment I envisioned her opening my pants and taking my cock into her mouth. I had yet to discover how skilled she was at sucking cock, but I could only imagine she was just as voracious and eager as she was at the fucking we'd already done. The thought of her tongue flicking over my flared crown had me shifting my cock in my pants. I had to push the thought of her mouth's sweet suction from my head. I knelt beside her and focused on our mission.

"We do not know if there are any Hive monitoring this level or any kind of motion sensors to indicate life forms," she said, her voice calm and even.

She was focused, although if she had that plug still in her ass, I doubted that would be the case. God, seeing that tight hole stretch around the plug made me—

"Remain here, I will investigate," she said, then shifted to move.

Focus!

I was used to the charge and conquer approach to fighting. A brigade of Atlan fighters was a force that even the Hive couldn't stand against. But Sarah wasn't Atlan and I had to continually remind myself that patience and strategy were required now, not brawn.

I grabbed her shoulder, stilling her. "We will do it together." I held up my wrist. "Remember, we can't separate."

"What if we get caught?" she asked.

I clenched my jaw. "We won't get caught."

"The first Hive we see I will… immobilize and we can claim their weapons and comm units."

"And then?" I studied her, smart enough to know that we were in her territory now. I'd never set foot on a vessel this small before coming to this sector. I hadn't survived a decade in battle by ignoring the knowledge or experience of my best fighters.

"The lifts are centrally located on all Hive ships, but there are access tunnels as well. I say we go for the tunnels. We'll have a better chance of taking them by surprise."

"Agreed."

She nodded and turned to work her way around the supplies.

Sarah

Seth was on this prison ship. So were other men, men who didn't deserve the fate that was in store for them. Hopefully, we would rescue all of them in time. Would Seth already be altered? Would he have the metallic skin and silver eyes of a soulless cyborg? Would he have the external attachments on his arms and legs? Would they shave his head? Inject him with microscopic implants in his muscles, making him faster and stronger than any human should be? Would he still look like my brother?

It didn't matter. As long as he was alive, I didn't care what he looked like.

Dax led the way, moving me aside when I would go first. Yes, he was a caveman, but in this moment he had two things that kept me from smacking him: the ability to rip the heads off a Hive without even warming up first, and a really fine ass. If a Hive appeared, Dax could go all berserker on them instead of firing. In the meantime, I would try to focus on rescuing my brother instead of the feel of Dax's butt in my hands. I knew how it flexed as he fucked me. Shit, I was in trouble. He was the only male in the entire galaxy who could distract me during a mission.

It hadn't even been two days and I'd changed so much. It wasn't the fact that I wasn't a coalition fighter anymore.

It wasn't that I'd been mated to an Atlan warlord. It wasn't even that my brother had been captured by the Hive. It had been the realization that I wasn't going to go through the rest of my life on my own. I no longer lived my life for someone else.

I'd joined the military because I was good at it, and I was good at it because I'd grown up with three older brothers who had given me no other choice. My father hadn't offered me princess dresses or a pony or even a prom dress. I had paintball wars, karate classes, and ice hockey. I'd never chosen any of those things, only following along and participating because I was the youngest, but also because if I hadn't, I would have been left out. Alone.

Then my dad threw the biggest life sucker of them all. A deathbed promise. I'd gone into the coalition because I'd promised my dad I'd find Seth and keep an eye on him. I'd been so focused on that I hadn't realized my dad had taken my entire life away. I had no choices. Nothing was my own. I just had to find Seth. I'd found him, fought beside him, but then he was captured. Once I pulled Seth from the Hive brig and transported him to safety, what then? Would I have to remain by his side forever? I'd done what my father had wanted and I would get Seth back to safe ground. I'd joined the coalition, left Earth. Hell, I'd even agreed to be a mate of an Atlan to keep my promise to my dad.

What was mine? What choices had I made in life that were all mine? Remarkably, it was Dax who made me see that there was someone who wanted me for me, who wanted what I wanted, was willing to do something for *me*. It was different, it was surprising. It was endearing.

This huge hulk of a space alien wanted what was best for me. Yeah, that included his acting like a Neanderthal—like now, when I had to remain safely behind him. He agreed to help me get Seth back because he knew it was important. He always checked to see if my head was in the right place before he fucked me, ensuring I was wet and eager for him. He even put that stupid plug up my bottom because he knew it would give me pleasure—even when I'd been completely skeptical. I was a little sore there now, but really, all my girl parts were sore. I hadn't been fucked like that in... well, ever.

His goal was to give me nothing but pleasure, so when this was over, when Seth was safe, I'd think long and hard about how I could please Dax. Not because I was told to do so. Not because I had to in order to be accepted by my mate, but because I *wanted* to know I'd made him truly happy.

Loud footfalls broke me from my thoughts. It wasn't a large group of Hive, probably the usual three. When Dax came out from behind a cube of supplies to fight them, I had a moment of panic that something would happen to him, but it was too short-lived to even get my heart rate up. Grunts and groans, an ion blast, hard metal striking the floor, a crash of a supply box as it tipped over, then quiet. Dax's breathing was ragged. "Clear."

I stood then and saw that there were indeed three Hive. Two were missing their heads and one had been shot. Dax reached down and grabbed a Hive weapon for me. It was slightly different than a standard coalition blaster, but after a few seconds of checking it out, I felt I could easily work it. I now had a weapon in each hand.

Dax's breathing didn't calm and I could see his heartbeat thrumming against the tight tendons in his neck. "Sarah," he growled.

My eyes widened. "What? What is it? They're dead, I'm safe."

He nodded his head, albeit jerkily. "It's... shit, it's the fever. Fighting these three brought it on."

"Then use it. Let's go get my brother, the others. On the way, you can rip the heads off as many Hive as you want."

"It's really strong. God, it came on so fast." He took a step back. I recognized that he was trying to protect me from himself.

I glanced around, realizing we were on a Hive prison ship and had to find Seth, but we couldn't go further until

Dax was back in control. I had to soothe him. I had to somehow get him back in control... I had to figure out something that didn't involve fucking. I wasn't going to get it on where we were. All was quiet, but it might not stay that way.

"I know. It's dangerous for us. I can't function like this, can't see who's bad or good. If your brother touches you, I'll kill him."

He'd warned me it would get bad, that the fever would be overpowering. But now? Here? A quickie might work, but neither of us would have our senses about us. Three Hive or three hundred could come upon us while he was fucking me and neither of us would know. Neither of us would even care.

I had to soothe him, but fucking was out. We didn't have time to stand here and linger either. I had to think and think fast or I'd be pressed up against the wall, my pants down and a cock deep inside my pussy. I got damp at the idea. Hell, I was already damp from staring at his ass.

Placing a weapon on a nearby box, I walked up to him and stroked his face. He hissed out a breath as he wrapped his arms about me.

"We can't fuck," I breathed as he ran his hands over me, even if I wanted it so badly my pussy ached.

"No," he replied, breathing raggedly.

"Kiss me," I said. "Touch me. I'm here. I'm with you. It's going to be all right."

I lifted up on my tiptoes so I could kiss him. Dax didn't resist, but met my mouth eagerly. His tongue instantly plundered as his hands roamed over my body; my hips, my ass, my breasts. It was easy to sink into the kiss because the feel of him, the taste of him was overwhelming. I was sinking fast, but I had to keep my head. I had to kiss him with all the pent-up need and desire I felt since we'd climbed from bed, but I had to be the one to pull back. Dax was clearly in charge when it came to fucking, but now, in this moment, I had to take the lead.

Pulling my head back, I rested my forehead against his. Our breaths mingled and we both were panting as if we'd run a marathon.

"Better?" I whispered.

"I love the taste of you. Your lips, your pussy," he replied, his voice rough.

"Calm that beast of yours so we can get Seth and get the hell off this ship. When we're safely back in our quarters, you can taste all of me."

I hoped the promise—and it was a promise—was enough to soothe him.

Dax growled deep in his chest. "Better," he murmured, then pushed me away from him. "You are forewarned that as soon as I get you alone and not on an enemy ship, I'm going to fuck you until you can't walk right."

"Noted," I said, my pussy clenching at the promise in his voice.

"Let's get your brother and get the fuck out of here."

As Dax led me to the nearest tunnel, I couldn't have said it better myself.

CHAPTER NINE

Dax

Sarah's kiss soothed the beast brought about by the Hive blood on my hands. The mating fever had come on so abruptly and so intensely that I'd been unable to stop it and had no way to tame it. I'd killed the three Hive without even blinking, but when I was done, I saw Sarah stand and knew I had to have her. The beast within wanted her with an intensity that was painful. I wanted to toss her over one of the supply cubes and fuck her, filling her again and again with my seed, my beast telling Sarah that she belonged to him. But not here, not now. And not on a Hive prison ship.

I couldn't even fuck her now. Sarah knew I needed something, and the kiss helped. Just being able to touch her, to feel that she was right there with me eased the harsh need. If she hadn't soothed me, kissed me, I would have been unable to stop the beast from taking control.

My breathing had calmed, my heart rate lowering. I could be near Sarah without the risk of hurting her. My mind cleared of the red haze of desire. Licking her taste from my lips, I was soothed. It was only temporary, but we were on this fucking ship for a short time. We weren't lingering.

As I came out onto the fifth floor, I turned to Sarah. She nodded and we went in. We didn't talk, we didn't even have to share commands. We knew exactly what we needed to do, trusting in the other.

There were three groups of Hive, easily wiped out. While the life sensors probably picked us up on their displays, we weren't staying. Sarah found the control panel and disarmed the doors on the holding cells.

"Seth!" she cried, stalking down the central corridor searching.

About a dozen men came out of the various holding cells, her brother one of them. The men looked worn, but well. Alive. Whole.

"Is this everyone?" I asked. A man looked around, took a head count, then nodded.

"Anyone too injured to walk out of here?"

"No. We're all ready," Seth spoke up and I nodded. Good.

"They were going to begin the transformation once we reached the IC. None of us have been touched."

I was relieved they had avoided true Hive horrors.

As Seth hugged Sarah, I ordered the other men to collect the Hive's weapons, to arm themselves for our extraction.

"What the hell are you doing with *him*?" Seth asked, glaring at me. It was fortunate he was not yet armed.

Sarah looked at the floor, then at me. "I'm mated to him."

Seth did then grab an ion pistol from one of the other soldiers and stormed over to me. "You mated her? Are you fucking kidding me? You landed in the middle of a battle and had me taken by the Hive! And now—" he ran his hand through his hair, hair the same shade as his sister's, "—now you drag Sarah back into dangerous territory, onto a fucking Hive prison ship? Are you an ass, or just stupid?"

I felt the tip of the weapon against my chest and I did not blame the man. He'd transported out of the battle before I'd said more than *Mine*. He hadn't heard that she was my mate, that I had claimed her. He knew nothing but the fact that I'd inadvertently fucked up their last mission.

"Seth, leave him alone. It was my decision to rescue you, not his. He tagged along to protect me."

Seth whipped his head around and looked down at his sister. "Are you kidding me?"

"If you are so worried about Sarah's safety, let's argue about this once we get back to the Karter," I said. "But your anger is to be directed at me, not Sarah. You will not raise your voice to my mate again."

He took a deep breath and let it out, but replied through clenched teeth. "Agreed."

Nodding once, knowing the one thing we had in common was Sarah's safety, I hit the comm unit on my shirt. "Battleship Karter. Respond."

There was silence. I repeated the call. The men glanced at each other, all at once nervous. If I'd been taken by the Hive and rescued, I would be nervous, terrified even, until I was safely back onboard a coalition ship.

"Transport room responding. Go ahead."

The men relaxed then, tentative smiles forming on their faces knowing they would soon be away.

"You have our coordinates, can track the fourteen coalition members. Transport."

"The magnetic storm that impacted your transport before has shifted. No transport. Repeat, no transport."

"How long?" I asked.

The men glanced about, clearly afraid of the Hive who would soon appear. The ship wasn't overridden with them; it was a prison ship and the enemy combatants were—until now—all behind bars. A large group of Hive was not needed.

"Unknown. Remain in place until we communicate. Out."

"Alternatives," Sarah called once the connection was broken.

The men considered and stated various options, but none removed us from this ship.

"We could fly out," Seth offered.

"Fly? This ship is too big. Besides," I added, "if we got it anywhere near a coalition vessel they'd shoot us out of space."

One of the soldiers offered a reasonable challenge.

"Every Hive ship has a flight deck with operational Hive squadron fighters. We can use one of those," another added.

"We'd still be blown to bits in a hostile aircraft," I added.

"Not if we flew past the magnetic interference, communicated with the Karter and transported from there," Seth offered.

I glanced at Sarah, who'd been listening intently. "I can't pilot a Hive fighter. Can anyone?"

The men shook their heads, but Seth looked at Sarah and grimaced. "Sarah can."

My eyes widened, completely unaware of this ability. She could shoot, kick ass, strategize, *fly*. What else could she do?

"I can't fly one of those!"

Seth wrapped his arms around Sarah's shoulders. "It's just like the C-130."

I had no idea what a C-130 was, so I had to assume it was an Earth ship.

"This is nothing like it," Sarah countered. "That's a supply plane. With wings and rudders."

"You are a pilot?" I asked.

Seth grinned, completely confident in his sister. "She can fly anything. You're her mate, shouldn't you know that?"

Sarah whacked him on the arm. "He's known me less than two days. Cut it out."

Seth offered me a dark glare but spoke to one of his men. "Meers, where is the flight deck?"

The recruit—his uniform showed only one bar on the sleeves—straightened his shoulders and responded, "Second floor, the aft end of the ship."

"We go there, get the ship. If you can't fly it, we're no

worse off than we are standing here in the middle of the brig." Seth looked between the men, then at me. "Warlord, you are the highest rank here."

"I am no longer a member of the coalition fleet," I replied.

"Got kicked out, did you?"

"Seth, leave Dax the fuck alone. If you don't shut the fuck up, right now, I'm going to leave your ass here. You get me? He's mine. I'm keeping him. Get over it."

Sarah defended me. From Seth. All this, everything we'd done since the first moment I'd seen her, had been about getting her precious Seth back. She'd only mated with me so that she could accomplish this task. Once we got off this prison ship, I'd have completed my commitment to her. I assumed she'd turn her back on me and want to handhold her brother through the remainder of her time in the service. Instead, she was defending *me* from *him*. She loved her brother. Did she now care for me as well? The idea puffed up my ego, surely, but it made me *feel* something besides the beast inside screaming *Mine*. It was my heart, my very soul that held hope. Not for a mate to fuck to end my mating fever, but a mate to keep because we truly wanted to be together.

Seth looked as if he'd rather eat some titanium bolts, but offered his sister a stiff nod. "Dax, you have the experience and skill of a warlord. We could use your input."

I eyed her brother for a moment. I had to admire his ability to suck it up when required. "I do not wish my mate to be in jeopardy a minute longer than necessary; however, remaining here is not a wise option. Flying out is valid, as long as Sarah can pilot the ship."

Seth's eyes widened at the term mate, even though we'd told him, and Sarah held up her arms so he could see the cuffs about her wrists. "Told ya so." She offered him a small smile and he just rolled his eyes.

"Then let's go," Sarah said, taking a deep breath.

I pulled Sarah to me and whispered in her ear, "Are you

sure?"

"Are you doubting me now?" Her eyebrows winged up.

"Hell, no. I'm questioning your brother's plan. If you don't think you can do it, we'll come up with an alternative."

She put enough stress on herself and obviously her brother heaped it on as well. I'd shown her she could share that burden—even if it was by spanking her—and I didn't want to lose the progress I'd made, the trust I'd begun to earn by pushing her too hard now.

"I flew in the military, the Earth military. Planes and space ships are not remotely the same though. I wasn't an astronaut, but I've got thirteen men to get off this ship. I went through some basic simulations during coalition training. I'll figure it out, or die trying."

"You will not die. We will find an alternative," I repeated. Just as she said, there were thirteen other men in this ragtag team. We could come up with another way or we could keep the Hive away until transport was possible.

She shook her head and looked me in the eye. "No, Dax. I can do this. I can get us off this ship. Trust me."

Before I could argue further, she started issuing orders. "Three of you take forward, three take our six. Ion pistols set to kill. Let's focus and get the hell out of here."

The men snapped into action, eager to get the hell off this ship, total confidence in Sarah.

We followed Meers and the advance guys to the flight deck. We encountered one Hive group, but we were able to quickly shoot them down.

There were two identical ships on the deck and Seth led us to the nearest one.

"Dax, Seth, keep the Hive off us while I figure out how to fly this tin can," Sarah said.

Seth grinned at her Earth term—I had no idea what a tin can was—and began to bark orders. I wasn't going to do Seth's bidding, but followed Sarah instead. She was my responsibility. I'd protect her, or, as she said, die trying. Of course, Seth probably knew that I wasn't going to do anything but flank my mate and didn't give me any commands.

We were halfway up the boarding ramp when the first sonar detonation threw us all to the ground. Ears ringing, I rose instantly, roaring a challenge. Three Hive stood on the opposite side of the launch pad, another set of sonar charges at their feet. The weapons created a small, contained blast radius that would disable the ship, or weaken the hull until it was no longer safe to fly.

I charged them, firing my ion pistol to take out the first before I reached them. The second collapsed as I neared, and I glanced behind me to find Seth on his knees, covering me. The third Hive calmly loaded a sonar blast as I neared, as if nothing existed but his mission, his need to fire his weapon at our ship.

I wondered what went through his mind when I cranked his head to the side, when his neck snapped. I would have continued, ripping his head from his shoulders, but Sarah was yelling at everyone to get onboard and Seth and I were the only two remaining outside the ship.

"Come on, warlord. Let's roll!" Seth yelled at me, shooting across the launch bay at another trio of Hive that entered on the far side of the area. I didn't have time to charge them and make it back to the ship, so I joined Seth and we hurried on board, closing the launch doors behind us.

The men slumped in the hallway, their energy drained by the escape and short fight. I located Meers. "Where is Sarah?"

"Pilot seat." He lifted his hand and pointed in the direction my mate had gone. Seth and I both took off at a run.

I found Sarah looking over the controls in the cockpit. She was buckled into the pilot's seat, a look of fierce concentration on her face.

"Well?" I asked. It looked like any other control board to me, but then, I was a ground fighter.

"The controls are unusual, more video game than cockpit, but I'll manage."

I didn't understand half of what she said, but it sounded promising. Shifting in the pilot's seat, she fiddled with the U-shaped steering column and odd foot pedals.

"There's no key to start the ignition sequence." She pressed a bunch of buttons until the displays came to light.

"Can you fly this?" I asked.

She continued to fiddle with the displays, flipping a few switches, then took a deep breath when the very powerful feel of the engines coming alive vibrated beneath us.

"Buckle up!" she yelled so those down the corridor would hear.

I glanced toward the back, but saw no one. Surely the men would know to get strapped in by now as the vibrations of the ship's systems were powerful and rumbled through the floor.

I did as she said, strapping the harness over my shoulders as Sarah mumbled to herself, a strange, repetitive chant I didn't recognize. "What are you doing?" I asked.

"Praying," she replied.

That didn't make me feel any better, but I had no choice but to trust in her abilities. I had to trust that when she said she could fly this ship, she could. I had to let go and give my faith and trust to Sarah. She was in control now. Everything in my body screamed at me to take over, to throw her over my shoulder and drag her out of here. But that was the primitive Atlan beast raging within, not the thinking man who sat beside her. An Atlan male never relinquished control in a dangerous situation. Never. And I began to understand what she'd given me, the depth of the trust she'd bestowed upon me in going against her own nature, in surrendering her body to me. Sitting powerless and helpless beside her was one of the most difficult things I'd ever had to do.

Ion blasts struck the pilot's window in bursts of white flares that scorched the glass.

117

"Hive at four o'clock," Sarah called.

"What?" I asked.

She pointed over my shoulder and I realized perhaps it was an Earth concept. Not true time, but... whatever.

"Two Hive groups are here," Seth yelled as he stuck his head in the cockpit.

Another blast hit the clear window. "No shit, Sherlock," Sarah said, her voice tense, her eyes on the display. "They're trying to overload the power grid, disable the ship."

A panel short-circuited to Sarah's left, so she reached over and shut it down.

"Get down so I can get us out of here!" she cried, her anxiety level clearly rising.

A blast shook the ship so hard I felt as if my teeth would literally shake out of my skull.

"Sonar detonators, too." Seth cursed as another blast caused several warning lights to ping from the copilot's seat. The blast of soundwaves would rattle our ship apart before we could even take off.

"This is why fighting on the ground is far superior." I looked for the ion blaster controls that would arm the guns mounted on the sides and front of the ship. I had no idea what I was looking at. I felt helpless, and my beast did not like the feeling. My muscles begin to pop, breaking open and growing larger as I fought to maintain control.

Sarah must have sensed my struggle because she called to me, her voice rock steady. "Dax, we're fine. You can't go all berserker in here, there's not enough room for that. So tell beasty boy he's just going to have to wait."

"Jesus. This is a fucking train wreck." Seth stepped to my side and pushed several buttons, the weapons on the top of the ship firing in the general direction of the Hive.

Another ion blast and I could smell burning circuits. The load roar of another sonar blast struck, then a pop. A warning alarm went off and I tried to figure out where to shut it down.

"Sarah, get us the fuck out of here," Seth yelled.

"Seth, get the fuck out of my face." Sarah gritted her teeth. "It's a good thing the Hive hadn't killed you, because when we get back to base I am going to do it myself."

She fiddled with a few more buttons and then hissed and grabbed her side.

"Get ready to go in…"

She pressed a yellow button. The bay doors opened, space beyond.

"Sweet baby Jesus, the doors opened," she muttered. "Three."

The steering control pulled back easily in her hands.

"Two."

Her knees moved as the pedals on the floor and wiggled the ship from side to side. She found the right balance of her feet and the ship leveled, floating off the floor in the launch bay, ready to accelerate.

"One."

She pushed forward on the steering column and the ship shot out of the prison ship like the rocket that it was. I was pressed back into my seat from the power of the thrusters, just fucking relieved to be out of there. Sarah, however, cursed like the worst Atlan brawler I'd ever heard, her movements jerky and stilted, as if she struggled to maintain control.

"Sarah, you can calm yourself, we are out of the ship's range of fire."

"I am calm," she replied, her words bitten off. I scented her blood in the air and reached for her, but she waved me off. "Give me a minute. I'm not done yet."

"You are injured."

She shrugged. "It's just a scratch, Dax. Leave me be. We're not home free yet. Talk to me, Seth."

Seth sat at a tracking station behind her, his eyes scanning for enemy ships that might be following us. "Looks clear. I don't see any pursuit."

"Thank God." She sat in silence, sweat sliding down her temple and her hands shaking as she directed the ship back toward coalition space. The magnetic field shook and rattled the ship for several minutes, and the tracking station's display became solid green.

Seth leaned back in his seat and pumped his fist in the air. "Yes. We're hidden by the magnetic field. They have no way to track us, sis! Holy shit! You did it!"

"Good. Dax, can you take the controls. Just hold it still—until we are…" Her hand dropped from the steering controls and she grabbed her side, doubling over with a moan. "Clear. Until we're clear."

Instead of looking out into space, I looked fully at Sarah. "I can still smell your blood, mate. And you're sweating like I've fucked you for hours."

Seth muttered something about hiding a body at that comment, but I ignored him.

Sarah grimaced but didn't argue. Something wasn't right. Her skin was pale. Too pale and her breathing was shallow, her eyes glazed over as she looked at me without seeing.

I removed my restraint and turned toward her. She blinked a few times and looked in my direction, but I knew she was no longer processing what she was seeing.

"Just a scratch, Sarah? Did you lie to me?" Moving slowly, I knelt beside her and got my first good look at her far side. I wanted to spank her and hold her at the same time the moment I did. Blood coated her armor and dripped onto the floor from a large piece of metal that was sticking out of her armor. The metal must have pierced a rib, possibly her lung. "You stubborn female. You're bleeding to death."

She glanced down at her side, placing a hand beside the shard of metal. "It's okay, Dax. It's better now. It doesn't hurt anymore." She grinned like a little girl, silly and carefree and I knew she was even worse off than I'd imagined.

"Seth, take the controls. Now! Meers!" I shouted down the corridor, undoing her restraints. Holy fuck, she was badly injured and she'd lied to me about it. She was bleeding to death and still flying a fucking Hive ship. Sacrificing herself to buy us a few more minutes. Dying for these men. For me.

"Stop yelling at me," she replied, resting her head against the pilot seat.

"You lied to me." I was frantic and my beast was raging. Not in need, but in fear. It was anxious, worried about our mate. It paced within me, alternately whining and roaring to be free, to tear this ship, and everyone on it, into pieces.

"Had to get you out of there."

"You are the most stubborn, difficult, annoying, frustrating female I've ever come across. You should have fucking told me how badly you were injured. When did this happen, Sarah? When?"

"Sonar detonator, when we were running onto the ship," she breathed. "It's all better though. It doesn't hurt anymore," she repeated, her hand on my forearm. She left a bloody handprint. If it didn't hurt, that meant...

"Sarah, you will not leave me," I whispered the command and pressed my lips to hers as Meers rushed into the small room.

"Yes, warlord?" Meers stuck his head into the cockpit as I pulled Sarah into my arms. Seth slipped into the pilot's seat, making sure to hold the control exactly where Sarah had been holding it.

"Sarah is gravely injured. Get the Karter's transport team on comms and get us off this fucking ship. *Now.* She dies, you all die with her." The threat was not an idle one. If I lost her before we got back to the battleship, the beast would tear every living being onboard this ship into tiny little pieces, and there wouldn't be a damn thing I could do to stop him.

• • • • • • •

"Damn suicide mission. The captain put your lives in danger with her reckless behavior," the ship's commander spouted.

"She saved twelve coalition fighters from the Hive *and* got you the Hive comms from the ship she stole." I straightened to my full height, towering over the Prillon warrior who dared insult my injured mate. "More than one man on this ship owes her his life."

The commander crossed his arms and shook his head. "I know. I'll take the men and the comms." The commander muttered his last words under his breath, but I had Atlan hearing, and the beast missed nothing. "Doesn't mean it wasn't reckless."

If I wasn't guarding my unconscious mate's body, I would have taken issue, beaten his face bloody. I was getting really tired of annoying commanders. First my own, who'd shoved me into the matching program so I didn't die, then Sarah's who'd refused to help her find Seth. Now, this one. I stood beside Sarah's emergency pod, watching as the doctors waved their wands over her wounds. I knew that the technology on this ship would heal her quickly, but my beast didn't care for logic or reason. I struggled with every breath to keep that darker side under control, for my mate had been injured gravely and there was nothing I could do. The doctors, yes, but me? I couldn't protect her in this moment. Now I had to stand by idly as the she was healed by the med control systems.

Seth and his men had worked comms and gotten us transported to a different ship, not the Karter, one that wasn't in direct line of the magnetic field. It had happened in all of five minutes, the men proficient in gaining assistance, but it had been that way my entire life. In the coalition fleet, everything had a reason and a purpose. Things made sense. Orders were given and followed. Every warrior was strong and knew exactly what was expected. We expected to fight, to bleed, to die. Every warrior knew his or her role, as did my Sarah.

I looked down at my mate and she appeared to be so fragile lying there, so weak and definitely not immortal. She was not a fierce female from one of the warrior races. No, she was just a delicate Earth woman who was my mate, my heart, my life. It didn't matter to me that she was a warrior now, so skilled she could organize a ground attack or fly an enemy ship through a magnetic field. She was braver than anyone I knew, smarter than any military strategist, and yet her body was so fragile. I actually ached to take her in my arms and carry her away from this place, from the men, the noise, the constant danger of an enemy attack. For years none of that had bothered me, I'd taken it as my due. We were at war with the Hive, had been since before my birth, and would likely be long after I was gone. Yet I did not want any of this to touch Sarah. No more. She was too beautiful, too perfect for the ugliness that surrounded her now.

I learned in those five minutes that I wasn't nearly as strong as I'd once believed. Muscles didn't protect me from the heartbreak of nearly losing Sarah. Where I was weak, she was strong. Her two brothers and father had died, her last remaining family transported by the enemy right before her eyes. Her response had been determination to save Seth. Her love, once given, was relentless in its strength, courageous and full of stubborn hope. Her love was the one thing I desperately wanted, and yet she guarded her heart so well.

It took those five minutes to make me see that we were a pair who had to compromise. She gave and gave and I took. It was time I gave as well, that I let her be herself, not force her to be the weak woman the commander painted her, and, admittedly, I'd first thought her.

I wanted to reach down and touch her, to feel her skin to ensure it was still warm, to feel her pulse, to watch her breathe, but the doctor had pushed me out of the way often enough already. When I threatened to rip his arms off if he had me removed from the medical center, he allowed me to stay as long as I didn't get in his way. It was a reasonable compromise, but I didn't take my eyes off her.

I wanted to spank her ass a fiery shade of pink for getting herself hurt, but she'd done nothing reckless to warrant it. I didn't want her in any kind of danger whatsoever, but I'd been right beside her when it had happened. There was no way I could have protected her, shielded her from the display console breaking or from the piece of that console now embedded in her side. Other than tying her to my bed, there was no way to completely protect her from harm. While I would ensure she enjoyed her time tied up, she would soon grow to hate the confinement and me. She could not be kept from her passion, her fighting, any more than I could. She was a warrior, and nothing I could do would change the heart of her. It was a harsh lesson I was learning, and unfortunately it had taken her being gravely injured to realize it.

How I would control the beast within as she put herself in harm's way, I had no idea. The doctor checked the display and moved to her opposite side. "I heard the captain saved the day."

I searched his face for insincerity, but found none. "She flew a damaged enemy craft off a Hive prison ship, evaded a triad of Hive recon fighters, and took us safely through a magnetic field. It wasn't reckless, it was a rescue."

"I agree with the warlord." Seth joined me beside Sarah and watched with a clenched jaw as she was tended. "And so will the other eleven rescued men whose lives she saved."

"She is going to be fine," the doctor told Seth. He'd met her brother already, but Seth had been sent to debriefing and had finally returned. "A sleep status will help heal the puncture wound. The computer says two hours and she will awaken. At that time, I will do a full medical exam to ensure she is completely recovered, but I have no concerns."

Seth gave one last look at his sister, clearly satisfied with her status, and turned to the head of the ship we'd transported to.

"Commander, with all due respect," Seth said. He faced the Prillon leader like the captain he was. Proud, tall. "All the coalition leaders chose to leave me and the others for dead. I'd be a Hive soldier right now if not for her. So you can fuck off if you're going to court-martial her. She had to deal with bullshit commands, then deal with this big beast and take care of me, too. She's Wonder Woman."

I frowned and so did the commander. "Who?"

Seth rolled his eyes. "A woman who can do it all."

I tried to hide my smile, I really did, for that described Sarah perfectly. I didn't know who Wonder Woman was either, but she was *my* Wonder Woman. I'd hated Seth at first for being the reason Sarah had to go back into danger, but I was liking him more by the minute.

"Captain Mills," the commander replied, his words gritted out through clenched teeth.

"Commander."

"I can't punish your sister because she's not part of the coalition army. She's *his* mate and I think that's probably punishment enough."

I would take offense but I was happily stuck with my little human mate. I just had to wait two hours for her to wake.

"As for you…" The commander pressed forward but Seth did not retreat. The two men stood practically nose to nose. While Sarah couldn't be punished by the coalition, Seth could be stripped of his command and forced into hard labor for the remainder of his stint. It was the commander's call. Seth had earned his punishment for insubordination alone. "Dismissed."

Seth saluted him and left.

"As for *you*," the commander turned to me. "Once she's healed, get your mate the hell out of here. Stop taunting me with what I can't have."

He spun on his heel and cut around the doctor, who'd returned to check on Sarah.

I smiled down at my mate. Her machines had a constant, even beeping and the doctor was calm and pleased with her response to treatment. I almost lost it when she'd passed out at the controls of the ship, not sure what to do. For the first time in my life, I wasn't in control. I hadn't had any way to save her. Muscles wouldn't do it. Brawn did nothing. Ripping someone's head off gave no solution.

And so I was forced to wait. Once she was healed, I'd spank her for scaring me so badly. Then I'd pleasure her because I loved watching her come all over my fingers and cock.

CHAPTER TEN

Sarah

I opened my eyes and saw Dax staring at me. I blinked once, then twice, trying to remember when I fell asleep. I was rested and comfortable, yet I felt as if I'd missed something.

"Feeling better?" he asked, a deep V formed in his brow.

"Feeling... oh!" I sat up then, barely knocking heads with him.

I was in a med unit with several beds and unconscious patients. I wore a gown, not unlike one worn in a hospital on Earth. It all came back to me: the prison rescue, the ship, the pain in my side, that piece of metal.

I put my hands on my side and saw that there was no shrapnel poking through my skin—or at least the gown—and there was no blood. It didn't hurt anymore either.

"You're all healed," he murmured, then stroked my hair back from my face. It was hanging free down my back.

"If this is how space medicine works, I like it," I commented, pressing against where I'd felt the searing burn from that puncture. If I were on Earth, I'd either be dead or I'd need weeks to heal. "How long was I out?"

"Two hours in the med unit, plus another five minutes being unconscious in my arms as your brother organized an alternate transport."

"That's all? Wow."

Dax rose to his full height then and placed his hands on his hips. "That's all?" he growled. I could hear the rumble deep in his chest. "Mate, do you have any idea what I've been through in that time?"

Before I could open my mouth, the doctor came over and began waving a funny wand over me. He kept his eyes on the display, then reached over and pushed a button on the wall behind me.

"You're free to go."

"I am?" I asked, completely amazed that I'd been stabbed by a piece of spaceship less than three hours ago and now I was fine.

"You are," he replied. "Fully healed and cleared from the med floor."

Swinging my legs over the side of the bed, I hopped down, my bare feet landing on the cold floor. I reached back and covered my bare ass that I knew was hanging out.

"She's cleared for *all* activities, doctor?" Dax asked.

I flushed, for I knew exactly what kind of activities he was referring to.

He cleared his throat. "Yes, *all* activities."

Dax bent down and before I knew what was happening, his shoulder was pressed into my belly and I was tossed over his shoulder. I put my hands on his lower back for balance.

"Dax!" I cried.

He spun on his heel and practically stalked toward the exit.

"My rear end is sticking out!" I could feel the cool air and knew *everyone* could see *everything*.

He stopped, gripped my gown and tugged it together, keeping one of his big hands on my bottom. I was thankful he was possessive, for we were down the hallway before I could think more.

"Where are we going?" I asked, watching the floor change color from green to orange, the only way I could tell from my perspective that we'd left the medical area and had entered the living quarters of the ship.

"To our room."

"Wait, the others. Are they well?" I asked. "Dax, put me down. I can't talk while I'm staring at your ass." I pounded it once with my fists.

"Everyone is fine."

"And Seth?" I held my breath as I waited for him to answer.

"Fine."

I sagged then, relieved. "Take me to him. Please," I added.

Dax paused at a junction of two hallways. "Very well."

He turned and walked down a long corridor and came to a door. Lowering me down, he wrapped his arm about my waist as he pressed the button, which on Earth would be called a doorbell.

I tugged at the gown. "You could have at least let me change before you carried me out of there. You really are a caveman," I grumbled.

"Wait until we return to our room." He gave me a pointed look. "Then you'll get to see what me being a caveman is really like."

The door slid open and Seth stood before me, clearly whole and well. Also clearly angry at Dax, for he couldn't have missed what he'd said about what he was going to do to me.

To stave off any latest verbal blows, I wrapped Seth up for a hug. It felt good to hold him again, to know he was safe and whole and... what? I loved him. I did. He was my brother and I looked up to him and listened to him and hated him when he was bossy. But...

I stepped back from the hug and looked back at Dax. He was looming there—there was no other word for the size of him just outside the doorway—waiting for me. He'd take

Seth's annoying behavior because I was his mate. Heck, he seemed to do *anything* for me. He'd gone into a Hive prison ship to rescue a man who hated his guts because I wanted him to.

Dax was the bossy one for me now, not Seth. He was the one whose hugs I wanted. He was the one who I worried about—not that I didn't worry about Seth, but *this*, this was different. *I* was different. I'd used Dax for my own gain, to get Seth back. I'd made a deal with him and he'd followed through with his end of it.

"I can't believe you mated with this hulk," Seth muttered. "Do you have any idea what you've gotten yourself into? I can't save you this time, sis."

My mouth fell open and I stared at my brother wide-eyed. Then they narrowed as I swear my blood pressure soared to stroke point. I stepped up to him and pushed my finger into his chest.

"Save me? Are you fucking kidding me? When the hell have you saved me?" I shouted.

Dax stepped into Seth's room and the door slid closed.

Seth looked uncomfortable now, running his hand over his hair. "From Tommy Jenkins in fifth grade when he wanted to look up your skirt. From Frankie Grodin when he only wanted to take you to prom so you could be another notch on his high school bedpost. From that jerk drill sergeant who made you do extra push-ups."

"First of all, Tommy Jenkins messed with me when I was ten and I punched him in the nose. Frankie Grodin had a rude awakening when Carrie and Lynn got a picture of him with his dick hanging out and emailed it out to the entire senior class. As for the drill sergeant, he made me do those extra push-ups because you kept coming to check on me. As for saving, who the fuck do you think saved your ass from the Hive, big brother?"

I crossed my arms over my chest, uncaring that the back of the gown was open and Dax could easily see my butt.

Seth turned redder and redder during my tirade and

pointed to Dax. "He landed in the middle of that fight and had me taken."

"He did, but that was an accident. Any one of the guys could have been grabbed. Hell, you could have been grabbed at any of the other battles we've been to. Why the hell are you pissed at him when he went in and rescued you?"

"Because he let you go with him!"

"So he should have gone in and saved you alone?"

We were shouting full out now and when I glanced at Dax, he was leaning against the wall with a smile on his face. For once, he wasn't butting in.

"He got you into this mess in the first place with that whole bride match thing." Seth waved his hand in the air as if he couldn't figure out what to call it.

"So us being matched is the reason all this happened? Jesus, Seth, you're a dumbass. If you want to blame someone, then go after Warden Morda back in Miami because she put me through the bride testing program instead of the coalition induction by mistake. You know what, you'd be perfect for each other."

I shook my head and exhaled a pent-up breath. Out of the corner of my eye, I saw Dax stiffen. Shit, those words probably pissed him off.

Seth's shoulders drooped. "I just want you to be safe. With Chris and John gone, that falls to me now."

I shook my head. "No, that falls to Dax."

I walked to Dax and wrapped my arms around him, pressed my cheek into his chest.

"I can see your bare ass, you know," Seth grumbled as he looked off to the side, clearly averting his gaze.

Dax's hand shot to my lower back and gripped the two sides of the gown together.

"Now I can see his hand on your ass."

"Jesus, Seth," I complained, then ignored him. I reveled in the hard feel of Dax, his scent, the lub-dub of his heart beneath my ear, even his hand on my ass. "All this mess made me see that I was living my life in your shadow, doing dad's bidding. I even went into the military trying to make dad happy, because of you and John and Chris."

He looked at me, completely surprised. "What? I thought you wanted to do that?"

"What, take karate at ten when everyone else was doing ballet? *That's* why I punched Tommy Jenkins in the nose, because I knew how to make a solid fist." I paused, then continued. "Look, Seth, I love you. I'm glad you did all that stuff with me, with Chris and John, but I've always been going through the motions, looking for what *I* want."

Seth tugged on his ear. "And what's that?"

"Dax."

I felt Dax tense beneath me, then relax. He spun me about so my back was to his front, his hands on my shoulders. I couldn't see him any longer, but I knew he literally had my back. I doubted he knew that Earth term, but the actual gesture was telling.

"Seriously?" Seth asked, shaking his head slowly.

"Seriously. I'm going to Atlan once his mating fever is finished."

"You are?" Both men asked the same thing at the same time.

"I am." I was. I felt good about it, too. "I don't need to be beside you for you to know I love you, but Dax does."

I felt a growl rumble against my back.

Seth waved his hand as he sighed. "Go, Sarah. All I ever wanted was for you to be safe and happy. That's all any of us ever wanted. Live happily ever after and have ten kids with—" Seth studied Dax for a minute, weighing his next words carefully as I balled my hand into a fist at my side, ready to punch him in the face if he insulted my mate one more time. "This very large warrior who, I'm sure, would die to protect you." Seth held out his hand to Dax, who looked confused.

"I would." Dax's deep, rumbly vow made my pussy clench beneath the robe and I heard Dax take a deep breath, drawing in the scent of my arousal. He growled then, pulling me closer. My brother stood silent and stoic with his hand out with his peace offering.

"Shake his hand, Dax." I pulled Dax's hand forward and placed it in Seth's so my brother could shake it. I smiled then, pleased to know that Seth understood. Maybe he, too, was looking for a mate.

Smiling, I wiggled my eyebrows at my brother in a suggestive manner. "You know, you're a captain now."

"I know." My brother released Dax's hand and looked confused.

"You can request a matched mate from the Interstellar Bride Program. She'd be perfect for you in every way, your perfect match."

Seth burst out laughing and I grinned, suddenly thrilled with the idea. Seth shook his head. "I don't think so."

"What, you afraid you're going to get a slimy, green alien wife?" I shook my head. "You won't. They test you, Seth. Hook your brain up to sensors and play mating ceremonies inside your head until you're so hot you think you're going to lose your mind. But they match you to someone who has the same kink in their head that you have in yours."

Seth looked from me to Dax, and back. "So you wanted big and scary, huh?"

Dax growled at him in warning, but I threw back my head and laughed as joy filled me. "Yes. I guess I did." I patted Seth on the cheek and grinned. "Now, if you'll excuse us, I need to tend to my space alien, for he's got a fever."

Seth groaned. "Jesus, sis, I don't need to know this shit. TMI." He went over to the door, opened it. "Go. Cure him. Whatever, but not in front of me."

Dax stepped forward then, once again his hand held out to my brother in an offer of friendship that surprised me. "I am taking my mate to Atlan, Seth. You will be welcome in our home any time."

Seth stared at the outstretched hand, then grasped Dax's forearm in a grip between warriors. "Take care of her."

"I intend to, starting with a hard spanking for lying to me about her injury, then… well, then—"

Seth released Dax's arm, holding up his hand as my mouth fell open at Dax's words. He was going to do what?

"Again, brother, too much information." Seth shook his head, chuckling as I blinked hard, trying to process what Dax had just said.

"You are *not* going to spank me," I sputtered, my cheeks heating. "I saved your life, Dax. I saved us all. If I'd told you how badly I was injured, you wouldn't have let me fly. You would have pulled me out of that pilot's seat and—"

Dax cut me off. "And found someone else to hold the damn controls still so you didn't bleed to death. You risked your life without reason, Sarah. You lied to me to do it. I will turn your ass a bright red so it does not happen again."

"You sure as hell better," Seth said, wearing that brotherly protective face. "You scared the shit out of me, too, Sarah." He nodded at Dax. "Add an extra swat for me."

Dax raised an eyebrow, but agreed immediately. "Done." He tugged me backward and out the door.

Before it closed, Seth said, "Warlord, if you hurt her, I will hunt you down and kill you."

Dax rubbed his thumbs over my shoulders. "I would expect nothing less."

• • • • • • •

Dax

A few hours later I stood on the balcony of our new home next to my mate and breathed in the scents and sights of Atlan. It had been ten long years since I'd seen the rolling gold and green hills, the towering trees with wide purple and green leaves, the flowers of every color that lined the streets like the most delicate spun glass, their transparent petals glistened beneath the light of our star like a million twinkling lights.

Beside me, Sarah looked breathtakingly lovely in a gown of the finest weave to be found in this sector. The pale gold draped from her lovely shoulders and molded to the tops of her breasts. It fit her curves to just past her hips before falling in a shimmering wave to sway just above her ankles. I reached around her and placed a large pendant around her neck, the oblong gold engraved, as our cuffs were, with the markings of my family line.

We'd arrive via transport, still wearing coalition body armor, Sarah's former rank as a captain on full display to the greeting party from the Atlan senate. The gasps and curious gazes had begun immediately, and I knew, even before our message comms began lighting up in the living quarters below, that my bride would be a celebrity here, a unique and intriguing woman who had fought beside her mate, a female warrior. Atlan might never recover.

She clasped the pendant to her chest and spun in a wild circle, laughing. I had never seen her so light and carefree. "I feel like Belle, from *Beauty and the Beast.*"

I frowned. "I don't understand what that means, mate."

She stopped and smiled up at me. "It doesn't matter. I'm happy. I've never felt like this before."

"Like what?"

"Beautiful. Soft." She spun again, watching her skirt rise in a flare around her knees. Her hair hung loose, the dark waves falling around her shoulders. "I feel like a princess. And we are living in a castle. Good God, Dax. Are you rich, or what? This place is ridiculous." Sarah smiled and threw her arms around my neck, lifting her face for a kiss, which I eagerly provided. When she was panting and breathless with need, when I could smell the sweet scent of her arousal, I set her back on her feet and looked down at the woman who was about to become mine in every way.

"Wealth is irrelevant here. I am an Atlan warlord, and you are my mate."

It was her turn to frown. "I don't understand."

I traced her cheekbone with my thumb, simply enjoying

her happiness, the carefree light in her eyes I'd never seen before. "Not many Atlans return from the war. Most are executed when they enter berserker mode in battle. Those who control their beasts, those strong enough to return, are rewarded with wealth, land, castles." I gestured to the massive structure surrounding us. The home was more than we needed, with nearly fifty rooms and a full staff of mated Atlan attendants to see to our every need. I traced her bottom lip, my cock growing harder with each passing second. "I am happy to provide for you, princess."

She inspected me then, taking in the formal dress of a retired warlord, the tight lines of the jacket that did not hide my massive chest or shoulders, the jacket designed to display the bright mating cuffs that encircled my wrists, that marked me as hers forever. Her smile faded and a dark, sad look stole the joy from her eyes.

"What are we going to do now, Dax? I don't know what to do if I'm not fighting. I feel worthless, like a bauble placed on the mantel left to collect dust. There are good men out there fighting and dying, and I'm twirling around like an idiot. I don't know how to be this—" She gestured at her gown and looked back up at me. "I'm not a princess, Dax. I don't know how to do this, how to be happy when I feel like I should still be fighting. When good men are still out there dying."

"They fight to give you this life. They fight so others can live full lives, just as you did for others with the coalition, and on Earth. I've been gone from Atlan a long time. We'll just have to figure it out together."

I yanked my jacket off and tossed it to the floor. My shirt followed. When I was bare chested, when I could feel her against my bare flesh, I pulled her close and settled her ear over my beating heart. "We will not be idle, mate. The senate will ask us to attend many events, acting as ambassadors for those thinking of joining the fleet. We will be interviewed and questioned by many. We will be consulted on matters of policy and war. We will teach others how to survive their coming battles, and we will have children, mate. I want my child growing in your womb. I want a houseful of rowdy boys and sassy girls. I want to have to sneak into the closet to fuck you, back you against the wall, and bury your cries of pleasure with my kiss so the children don't hear your screams."

Her shoulders shook as she laughed. "You are so bad, Dax."

I lowered my hands to her back and unfastened her dress, letting the soft fabric fall to pool at her feet. I knew what she wore beneath, a thin sheet of clinging fabric that would not stop me from spanking her, fucking her, claiming her.

I lifted her then, cradling her in my arms and walked back inside our bedchamber, settling on the side of the bed with her in my lap. She lay quiet and content, her warmth a balm to my senses. Having her here, in our new home, settled me in a way I'd never imagined possible.

And yet, there was still a lesson to teach.

Lifting her head with a finger beneath her chin, I kissed her until she melted, until her arousal soaked the thin dressing gown she wore and her nipples were hard peaks beneath my exploring hands.

When she was soft and pliant, I flipped her over so her stomach was pressed to my thighs, her head hanging down and her ass lifted in the air for a firm spanking.

"Dax! What are you doing?" She squirmed, but I held her down with one strong hand on her back.

"You lied to me, Sarah. I promised you a spanking. It is long overdue as we were rushed through transport."

"Dax. No. You can't be serious about that. I had to—"

My firm hand striking her ass stopped her argument. She cried out, not in pain, but in outrage and I struck her again, harder this time, making my palm sting with the force of my strike. "No, mate. You do not lie to me. Ever. You will speak the truth. You will learn to trust me."

Smack!

137

She kicked as I continued, "If you had trusted me, I would have helped you. I could have tended your wound, taken your direction to fly the craft, prepared a med kit for you." *Smack!* "Instead, you stole my right, as your mate, to care for you. You endangered yourself, the men we risked our lives to rescue and me. You lied to me." *Smack!* "Never lie to me again."

She pushed at me, but she was small, her arms not long enough to gain purchase on the floor. With a snarl I ripped the transparent fabric from her body, the thin material parting in my hands like paper as I bared her to me and struck again and again.

Silence reigned, broken only by the sound of my firm strikes on her bare ass. She did not cry, argue, or beg for leniency. I struck until her ass was a bright red, until I heard from her what I needed to hear.

"I'm sorry, Dax." Her voice was a whimper of contrition. "I shouldn't have lied to you. I should have told you the truth and trusted you to help me. I'm sorry. I didn't mean to scare you. I honestly didn't understand."

"Understand what?"

"How much you—care for me."

With her words, my will to continue her punishment bled from me and I rested my hand over her soft skin, petting her, needing to touch her, to know she was safe and healed and mine as she lay quiet and accepting of my touch. "You are my life, Sarah. You are everything."

Not wanting to wait for a response to my confession, to be disappointed by her lack of feeling for me, I reached to my right and found the small box exactly where I'd left it on the bed. Holding her in place with my hand spread across her lower back, I removed the sexual device from its resting place and picked up the lubricant I would need to ensure her pleasure. I would make her come until she thought of no other, longed for no other life. Eventually, she would love me. For now, she was here, naked. Mine. It was enough.

"Do not move." I barely recognized the growl of my voice, realized that the beast would not be denied, not this time. "You are mine."

"Dax? What are you—"

With a swiftness and precision born of need I worked the lube and the plug into her tight ass; the sight of the control switch sticking out of her bottom actually made me growl.

"Mine." It was the only word I was capable of speaking at the moment, my head filled with it, with the need to fuck her, claim her, fuck her again. I needed the scent of her pussy coating my cock, I needed her cries of pleasure in my ears, I needed the soft feel of her submissive body beneath my hands and my bonding scent rubbed into her skin.

"I might be yours but why did you stick that thing in my ass?" She squirmed and it only made my cock harder.

"That *thing* is to bring you pleasure. Remember, it is my job to punish you, but also to bring you pleasure."

I pulled her ass cheeks apart, inspecting the placement of the pleasure device as well as the glistening, wet folds of her pink pussy. She was soaking wet; the scent called to the beast in me, a scent I could not ignore.

"I don't need you to put something… *there*."

I gave her one gentle swat to her already pink ass. "Yes, you do. The last time, you loved it. Remember, we are mated and I know what you need. You *need* this and I will give it to you." I tapped the base of it once and she gasped. "You will love it."

In one swift movement, I lifted her hips, rotated her body so her stomach pressed to mine, and brought her pussy to my eager lips. She cried out, her legs flailing for a moment before her knees came to rest on my shoulders, but I ignored the sound, desperate to taste her again, to fuck her core with my tongue.

Invading her body, I welcome the transformation I felt flow through my own. My muscle cells burst and reformed, larger, stronger. My gums receded and I felt the fierce tips of my teeth as I licked her pussy from front to back, hard, swirling the tight tip of my tongue over and around her clit, over and over again until her thighs tightened around my face and she whimpered, pushing against me with shaking hands.

Sucking her clit into my mouth, I growled then, low and deep. Loud. So loud that I knew the vibrations of it could probably be felt down the long corridor, and the reverberations would strike her clit like a sonar blast, forcing her over the edge.

Sarah's whimpered cries pleased me as her pussy pulsed with her release. I shoved my tongue deep, riding out the storm of her orgasm, stroking the inner walls of her body hard and fast, drawing out her pleasure.

When it was over, I stood, swinging her body up and around in my arms in a circle, until I had her mouth beneath mine, her breasts crushed to my chest, her tight, wet pussy inches from my huge cock.

She drew back with a shudder and looked me over, from the bulging size of my shoulders to the elongated features I knew now marked my face. I expected fear, shock, repulsion. But her eyes simply widened and she fought for breath. "Holy shit, you're hot, Dax."

"When this night is through, you will be mine. We will be bonded, mated, joined. The fever will be gone and all that will remain is you and me. You'll be mine forever, Sarah. I will never let you go."

Her eyes flared at my possessive words and I watched as a shiver raced over her body. I shook with the need to let my beast free. Perhaps she sensed it, for she lifted her chin in challenge.

"Make me yours, Dax. You're still holding back."

Sweat dripped from my brow onto her breast and I leaned down to lick her dry, to trace its path between her cleavage before working my way back up to her neck. I nibbled there, holding her perfectly still in my arms as she squirmed to get closer.

"I don't want to hurt you," I admitted. "I don't know what the beast will do." It was on a short leash, tugging and yanking to be set free, ready to fuck hard.

"You'll never hurt me." She leaned her head back, giving me—no, giving my beast the gift of her exposed neck, her trust.

I shook my head and squeezed my eyes closed. Spanking was one thing, but I'd never given my beast free rein before. "You can't be sure."

"Dax," she whispered, then waited for me to open my eyes. "I can be sure. You won't hurt me. Your beast, it won't hurt me either. We're mated, remember? *You* might know that I really like a plug in my ass."

Her cheeks flushed bright pink at her admittance.

"But *I* know that you would *never* hurt me." She swallowed, licked her lips, then continued. "I want it. I want you. I want both of you. Let him out, Dax. I want to meet your beast."

That was the last of my control. With those words, I snapped, the beast breaking free and I roared. My cock throbbed and pulsed, thickening even more, ready to fill her. I felt my muscles shift again, my body enlarging with agonizing pain. Sharp teeth pricked my lower lip and I could feel my hands shifting curve and angle so I could grip her better, hold her still as I took her. There would be no escape for her.

"Dax." Trembling fingers traced the harsh angles of my face, but the beast did not smell fear, which was a blessing. I was beyond the point where I could offer comfort or ease her doubts. My beast was in full command now, and he only had one answer for everything.

"Mine."

She wiggled in my arms, reaching up to kiss me. "Yes. I'm yours."

The beast growled, but liked her answer, like the soft press of her lips to mine. I walked forward without speaking another word, taking her to a padded wall where I knew I could take her the way I wanted to without hurting her. The beast always fucked standing, never laid down, never let down his guard. It was the Atlan way and the room was prepared for it. "Mine."

"Yes." Her back hit the wall and I pulled her ass cheeks wider, spreading her wet pussy open wide above the head of my cock.

"Mine." I impaled her against the wall in one hard, fast thrust. She was so hot, so wet, so fucking tight I nearly exploded, the plug in her ass rubbing the base of my cock with each stroke. My existence narrowed to her: her eyes, her scent, her soft cries and softer skin. The wet pussy waiting to take my seed. "Mine."

"Oh, God." Her words did not please my beast. *I* was her only god now.

"*Mine!*" The beast thrust harder, his growl fierce and unyielding as I buried my cock as deeply in her pussy as I could go. Holding her in place with my body, I lifted her arms over her head and attached the cuffs to the magnetic locks in place above her. She tried to lower her arms, then gasped as I lifted her legs and plunged into her again and again, lifting her hips higher on the wall with each thrust.

I did not relent through her first orgasm, fucking her harder and faster as she moaned and whimpered before me. I could do this for hours, and would, until my beast was satisfied. I fucked her hard, her knees draped over my elbows so I could hold her legs open, wide open. With each thrust of my cock her breasts jiggled and danced just for me. Her eyes drifted closed, the strained lines of ecstasy creased her face as she came again, as her pussy clamped down on my cock like a vise. The sight was mesmerizing and I knew I would kill to protect her. My loyalty belonged to her alone, not king or country, not to any planet or family line. I belonged to her. Only Sarah. "*Mine.*"

Sarah cried out her pleasure once again as my beast roared with joy. It was going to be a long night and Sarah was going to love every minute of it. We would be truly connected now, soul deep. Nature took over and started the bonding process, the scent of my bonding pheromones filled the air around us and I pulled her head close to my skin, ensuring she breathed in my scent, marking her flesh, scenting her, making her mine at last. The beast growled in agreement as she nipped at my chest.

CHAPTER ELEVEN

Sarah

With my arms locked above my head, a giant I barely recognized taking me with my back against the wall, the strong scent of musk and man invaded my senses until I was drunk on the smell of his lust, his flesh. He pulled my head close to his chest and I rubbed my cheek there, eager to revel in the call of my mate. He smelled better than any cologne I'd ever imagined. He smelled fierce and dominant, safe and mine. I nipped at his chest, hard enough to appease my own need to mark him, to claim him as he claimed me. And holy shit, was he claiming me!

When I heard the growl I knew he was mine. *Knew.* The fact that he held out this long was proof of his strength, even over his hidden beast, but no longer. He was mine. His *beast* was mine.

Yes, beast. That word had once scared the crap out of me, for hello? A beast? When the growl practically shook an orgasm right out of me, I knew it had been unleashed.

He thrust into me and I thrilled at the taking, the thick shaft that filled me, the inhuman strength that held me shackled for his claiming as he thrust again and again, deeper and deeper until I felt like he'd climbed inside my soul, until I knew I'd never get him out.

I had wondered what this moment would bring. Would he be like a rabid dog, foaming at the mouth? Would he be like those animal shifters I'd read about in romance books? Would he be crazed and hurt me?

He ground his pelvis against my clit and I moaned in need. No. He would never hurt me. The knowledge bloomed in my chest even as he held my legs open and plunged into my core, deep and hard, rubbing his skin against mine, rubbing his scent all over me. He was bigger like this, his muscles nearly bursting from his skin. He seemed unreal, like a comic book hero with bulging muscles and sharply defined features, as if his face had been stretched as well. His teeth appeared longer, and pure predator, capable of ripping out my throat as easily as he tasted me there now, his lips and tongue exploring me instead, making me shiver.

This side of him simply made him more virile, more male, more *Dax* than ever before. The way he was looking at me, I knew he wanted me. While his beast may want my body, I could still see hints of Dax, too, and he wanted *me*. We'd fucked, no, we'd made love before, we'd shown each other how much we needed each other by touch, by feel, by pleasure, but always he'd held himself in check, hidden this side of his nature from me. But no more. Now I would get the best of both sides of Dax. His cautious, gentle side and… this, his wild side, too.

Dax still had control and while he'd linked my cuffs to the wall above my head, and I was truly at his mercy, he did not harm me even when the beast took over and he filled me completely. He sped up his pace and I cried out, arching my hips at the feel of him. He swelled within me, even bigger than before. So thick and hot, a beast that had invaded my body without mercy or apology. I shifted my hips to take him all. He wasn't hurting me, but I had to bite my lip to keep the cry locked in my throat as I adjusted to the additional stretching, the erotic burn of his conquest, the pain of his tight fists on my tender bottom driving me higher, hotter, wilder.

My orgasm rushed through me and he bellowed as he found his own release, his cock pulsing and moving inside me, coating my insides with his hot seed. He stilled, his breathing ragged as he held me still, rubbing my skin to his, scenting my flesh and tasting me with his kiss. He said the one thing he seemed capable of in this form and I smiled. *Mine.* Over and over.

"Yes," I said, licking my lips. He pulled back to look at me, his muscles shrinking, his face returning to the form I'd come to adore as he stroked my cheek with his thumb and held himself still. A vein pulsed at his temple and sweat trickled down the side of his cheek as his breathing calmed, but he did not release me from his hold. He did not pull his cock from me, or settle my legs on the floor. I remained as I was, pinned to the wall by his cock, held in place for his pleasure as his dark eyes roamed my face and body, inspecting every inch.

"Are you all right?"

"I'm fine." He didn't look reassured, so I added, "I wanted you, Dax. I wanted your beast." I clenched my inner walls, squeezing him for emphasis, shocked to discover he was still erect.

His eyes flared then as he felt my intimate gesture and he shifted his hips, thrusting again as I moaned. He groaned in return, plunging again, claiming my mouth in a kiss that arched my back off the wall, my inner walls eager for more.

"Are you truly well? I didn't hurt you?" he growled.

I tugged at the cuffs just to hear them rattle, to remind myself that I couldn't do anything but submit and let Dax and his beast do what they wanted with me. "Yes."

Craning my neck, I tried to force his lips back to mine, attempted to entice him by once more squeezing his cock.

He kissed me, hard. "Do you want more?"

"Yes."

"Beg me, Sarah. Say my name. Say it." The words were like a whip, quick and sharp.

"Dax, please." Meeting his gaze, I continued. "Please. Hard, rough. Again and again. Let go, Dax. Let the beast free. *I want you.*"

He looked me over one last time, then finally... finally relented for good. I loved him all the more for his concern for me, but it was time for him to let go. "Yes, yes, I think you do."

He took me then, hard and fast. There was no gentleness, no rhythm to his masterful strokes. He fucked and he fucked thoroughly until another release melted my insides and I fought for air.

I thought he was done, that surely the fever was burned off, but no. With hands that were gentle, he released my wrists and carried me to the bed before turning me onto my stomach, rearranging me just as he desired. He slid a pillow beneath my hips and stroked my hair back from my face. I couldn't move, was too replete, too sated to do anything but let him have his way.

"Are you ready for more, Sarah?" The man's voice had fully returned, the lover I recognized, the man I would give anything for, would die to protect.

"Dax." I whimpered at the idea of being taken again. Another intense orgasm, another chance for him to dominate my body, my very spirit. "Yes."

He stroked his big hands down my arms, over my shoulders, down the length of my spine. Only then did he slip his fingers lower and into my still wet pussy.

"Here, Sarah. I want you again. My beast is satisfied, for now. But worried that we hurt you."

"I'm fine."

He stroked over my clit and I shifted on the bed, pushing into his touch as he spoke. "I need to take you again. Will you let me?"

I appreciated his care, but sometimes a girl loved being shoved up against a wall and fucked like she was the most beautiful, irresistible, desirable woman in the world. "You and your beast, Dax, can do whatever you'd like."

He laughed, then leaned over me, turning on the vibrations in the butt plug as he'd done that first night. I moaned with need as the new, different sensations awakened my desire once more. He lifted my hips from the bed and slid behind me to kneel between them, pulling my ass high in the air. He gave a sharp slap to my still sore bottom and I gasped, shocked as heat scorched my insides. Before I could react, he struck the other side and heat raced to my clit. I was about to beg him to fill me when he finally pulled me backward and up, onto his thighs as he shoved his cock deep, sliding inside me from behind.

He moved slowly, kneading my sore bottom, pulling the lips of my pussy open wider, exploring our intimate connection with big, blunt fingertips, spreading me open as he slid in and out of my core, completely open for his inspection as he watched his cock slide in and out of my body. My face was pressed to the soft bedding, my thighs shoved wide, my ass and pussy his to master... and I let him. I surrendered everything, content to be taken. I'd never felt so powerful as I did in that moment. It could have been five minutes or an hour, I lost track of time as he moved in and out of my body with deliberate control, staking yet another claim. If the beast had taken me minutes ago, Dax took me now, the man. This was my partner, my mate. He reached beneath me to rub my clit, pulling the plug on my ass at the same time, gently fucking me with it as well. I knew what he wanted. He would force more pleasure from my overly sensitive body, he would demand and I would give him what he needed.

"Come for me, Sarah. Come now."

My body responded as if on cue, the orgasm rolling through me as soft mews of pleasure escaped my throat. He spilled his seed in me as I came, and I felt like a goddess, a beautiful, desirable sexual goddess who'd just tamed a beast.

• • • • • • •

I woke wrapped in Dax's embrace, his body molded to mine—my back to his front. I could feel all of him, every inch of his naked form wrapped protectively around me. He slept peacefully and I felt like I'd conquered the world, happy that the beast inside him was finally satisfied. We weren't just mated now, but bonded; his scent surrounded me, drifted from my own flesh and made me feel safe, sheltered, like I belonged. I was sore, deliciously sore between my legs. A frozen bag of peas would come in handy, for while Dax had been as considerate as he could, his cock was... substantial and he hadn't been exactly gentle.

Smiling, I let the memories of last night play over in my mind. He'd been demanding, dominant, and I wouldn't have it any other way, grateful for the lingering soreness that kept me from forgetting Dax's power, the wildness that lurked within him. I saw the shine of one of my cuffs, noted that they matched the pendant around my neck, and sighed with contentment, knowing they were the only things that adorned my body. I raised my arm so I could look at a cuff. I touched it, felt the warm smooth metal, traced its design with one fingertip, my mind a sudden jumble of curiosity. I had no idea what it was: gold, titanium, some kind of Atlan mineral. The snugness of it, once a curse, was now a happy and very obvious reminder of our deep connection.

I traced the pattern over and over as I thought of the incompetent human woman, Warden Morda, the mouse, and how her mistake had led me here, to this bliss in the arms of a man I loved. Dax was honorable and brave, dominant and virile. He was strong enough that, for the first time in my life, I felt safe leaning on a man, depending on him for comfort, for care, for love. I was mated to an alien a bazillion miles away from Earth, and I felt freer than I'd ever been before. Free to be myself, to dance and wonder and dream. Free to fall in love and stop fighting for money, respect, survival. Years of tension and worry were gone thanks to the Atlan warlord sleeping next to me.

"You can remove them now," Dax murmured.

I stilled at his words. I didn't want to remove them; they marked me as his mate. I didn't want anyone to ever question our connection. He was mine. Had I been mistaken? Now that his mating fever was gone, did he plan to walk away from me? From us? He could live a long, happy life now with some meek, mild Atlan woman. Had I served my purpose? Was that all I was to him, a means to an end now to be discarded?

The thought was like a knife stabbing through my heart and I realized how truly far I had fallen. I loved him all right, with every ounce of fire and passion in my body. I'd surrendered everything last night, heart and soul, and it was too damn late to try to take it back.

"Turn this way, Sarah. I'll help you take them off."

"I didn't realize you were awake," I commented instead, turning my head away so he would not see the hurt his words caused, the unease.

"Mmm. Your breathing changed. You're upset." His large hand traveled the curve of my hip and waist as if he gentled a wild animal. "What troubles you?"

Curling into a ball, I kept my back to him, unsure what I would see on his face if I turned in his arms, unable to bear the thought that I might see disinterest, or regret. "Nothing. Go back to sleep." I could sneak away if he no longer needed me. Surely someone in the main house could help me remove the cuffs. I'd leave them for his new Atlan bride, the quiet, serene woman he truly wanted.

The gentle glide of his hand turned to a sharp snap of pain on my bare bottom and I yelped as he turned me to face him. "You're lying to me again. I thought we discussed that."

Determined to maintain what little dignity I had left, I held back the tears that burned in my eyes and studied his handsome face. He looked truly relaxed for the first time since I'd known him, the ease making him appear younger, less fierce. A small smile played at the corner of his mouth as he leaned forward and kissed me once, softly, before pulling back with raised brows. "Are you going to tell me what's bothering you, or do you require another spanking?"

"I—"

"I know every part of you, Sarah, as you know me. There are no secrets between mates."

I stroked my finger down his cheek. "A girl has to have some secrets," I countered.

He gripped my wrist directly over the cuff.

"Not with me. This cuff, it served a purpose. It freed you from the coalition so you could go after your brother and come to Atlan, with me. It kept us together until the fever was broken, keeping my beast in check until it was safe to free him. Now... now they are no longer needed."

I frowned then, surprised that he'd spoken so directly to my fears. "Are you saying *I'm* no longer needed?" The stab of pain spread from my heart up my throat to my head where it lodged behind my eyes, squeezing them in a relentless, fiery grip. Tears gathered and I could not stop them from spilling onto my cheeks.

Dax shifted on his pillow and lifted one hand to capture a stray tear on his fingertip. "Woman, you are indeed crazy. I've said the same words over and over and over. You are my mate. Mine. How many times did I say it last night? You. Are. Mine. I am not giving you up. I am not letting you go. Not ever. I don't care if you wear the cuffs or not, you're mine. You'll always be mine. I've fallen in love with you. I will not allow you to rid yourself of me."

"Then why... why do you want me to take them off?"

He wrapped his large hands around the cuffs and pulled them forward to settle over his heart. "I want you to stay beside me because you want to, not because the cuffs require it."

My big battle-hardened beast. I cupped his sharp jaw and smiled, letting all the love I felt for him shine brightly in my eyes. "I love you, Dax. I don't know how it's possible after such a short time, but I do. I love you. And after what we did last night, I don't think you have to worry about me going far. I'm going to want your beast to take me again… soon."

Cupping the back of my head, he kissed me slowly, as if he had hours. When he finally pulled away there was a sparkle in his eye I'd never seen before. "You only want me for my cock then?" he teased.

"Mmm. Definitely. I want all of you." I swallowed my pride and my fear and told him exactly what I wanted. "And, I want to keep the cuffs on."

His eyes widened in surprise. "That means you can never be far from my side, you can't go off on any wild adventures. You'll have to be next to me, close, always."

I shrugged, trying to act casual when what he described sounded like heaven to me. "Isn't that what Atlan mates normally do?"

He nodded. "Yes, but I did not dare hope you would agree to such a thing."

"Don't you want me close to you?"

"Always." The word was a vow, and the sincerity behind that one word shocked me to my core as tears fell from my eyes for an entirely different reason.

I traced his lips with my fingertips, doing a little teasing of my own in a vain attempt to hide how deeply his promise affected me. "We wouldn't want that big, bad beast to come out to play without me around."

He rolled over me and I lay back, happy to open my legs to him, to the hard probing heat of his cock. He pressed me into the bed, his hard length sliding slowly into my awakening body as I came to life, hot and wet and ready for him. Buried deep, he held himself up by his forearms so I could only see his face, could only look into his dark eyes as he filled me, shifted within, made me sigh with pleasure as I wrapped my hands around his neck and my legs around his hips, pulling him closer.

"Dax, I'm afraid that beast of yours is a terrible problem. He needs to be tamed."

Dax lowered his head and kissed me like I was the most precious thing in his world, and when he spoke next, I believed every word.

"No, mate, you've already tamed us both."

THE END

21653950R00090

Printed in Poland
by Amazon Fulfillment
Poland Sp. z o.o., Wrocław